Also by Reece Willis

Towards the Within

Praise for Towards the Within

'Life altering and personally insightful'

'One of the best books I've read in a long time'

'Heartbreaking, adventurous and written from the soul'

'An ending so unexpected I basically gasped'

What
We
Become

REECE WILLIS

Published by Worldworx Publishing 2020

www.worldworx.com

A catalogue record for this book is available from the British Library

ISBN: 978-1-9164301-3-6

For more information on Reece Willis visit www.reecewillis.com

For Catherine,
who saved me from myself

1

Even the air-conditioning is irritating, but that's a modest underlay to the rest of the noise that is threatening eruption. The relentless opening of wrappers from my neighbour, an elderly lady who offers up a boiled sweet with a smile each time she delves into the packet; the grating voice of the captain updating our journey every few hours; the constant din of my fellow passengers and the chinking wine bottles that beckon my fractured sobriety. Worst of all, the new-born girl screaming for attention in the seat ahead has me gripping my armrest until I can take no more. I get up, stagger to the toilet, and avoid the stares as I pass by until I lock myself in the cubicle seeking the safety of solitary confinement if only for the five minutes it offers. It must appear as if I'm suffering from travel sickness the number of visits I make throughout the duration of the flight.

When the announcement finally comes that we will soon be landing in Bangkok, I unclip my seat belt ahead of the overhead warnings that instruct me otherwise and fidget with my shoulder bag, chewing my tongue with the promise that this will soon be over. Despite the freedom on the other side of the airport I wait for the plane to empty before passing seat upon seat littered with discarded blankets, magazines, empty water bottles and cellophane packets that once held the standard issue headsets, now stuffed into the seat pockets, or left as trip hazards in the aisle. The weary stewardesses bid me farewell and I join the rush of an abrupt standstill of tapping feet at passport control.

The taxi driver, looking no older than twelve, grabs my backpack as I step out into the intense heat, hauls it into the trunk and flashes me a line of stained teeth, 'Where you go?' I tell him the address of a cheap hotel I've booked. He stares at the confirmation print-out and says he knows.

'First time Thailand?' he says cheerily into the interior mirror.

'No,' I lie and remove my journal to study my notes in the hope he'll give up.

'Very good time of year come to Thailand. How long you stay?'

I glance up and then down to the saviour of my phone hanging loosely from my trouser pocket and put my earphones in, cutting him off with Kings of Leon's *Closer* before he has another chance at his niceties. His mouth continues to move as his eyes dart from the road to the mirror to see if I've heard. I wind the window down to allow the sewage and diesel fumes to carpet my lungs.

Skyscrapers appear, sweep past and change direction as we speed over the flyovers and along the highways to meet an endless car park of traffic chugging an inch at a time. When we finally arrive at the run-down hotel on the corner of a litter plastered street, he lifts my backpack from the car and exchanges it for the relevant fare.

'Sawadee ka,' the cheery receptionist greets me as I enter, hands held together as if she's about to pray.

I pass her my confirmation slip, credit card and passport. Key in hand I head towards the elevator. Two giggling girls in their mid-twenties appear as the doors swish open and carelessly knock into me in their eagerness to get out and explore. I press the button for the third floor, relieved to rise above the deafening cackle. Inside my room, with the door closed behind me, I let out a sigh. I'm not even sure what I'm doing here. I look at my heavily scrawled notes, then close the journal. Catching my reflection in the mirror I realise I desperately need sleep.

Outside, the sun strikes an unbearable white into my retinas, silhouetting the tangled mass of cables scrawling above. The traffic slips past without a break. I carry on along the worn-out pavement, past food vendors fanning vomit-inducing smoke into the sky until the brief lapse in motion allows me seconds to cross. I'm accosted by taxi and rickshaw drivers, but I ignore them until I'm hopelessly lost and give in to one who won't stop pitching, trailing me with his sales patter. I instruct him to take me to the hotel where she's staying.

On the opposite side of the street is a coffee shop with seats outside that afford a clear view of the extravagant hotel entrance. I take up my position, unaware of whether she's in or out. Every now and then I glance down to my cup, my accumulating thoughts intensifying my adrenaline. When I pass the third hour, the novelty of my presence wears thin on the waiters, the elongated length between orders souring their patience. As I settle the bill, I catch a glimpse of her blonde hair before it's swallowed by the revolving doors. The world around me stops and I'm transported back to so many days all at once, my entire consciousness consumed by choices I made and could have made to make that alternative difference. Could I have held on to her with different hands? Protected her from those decisions that were all my doing? They say hindsight is a wonderful thing, but it's haunted me for so long now, it's all but eroded my soul. I look upon her in my mind's eye, at her new life so far removed from mine and I feel helpless, a hostage of my own guilt with no bargaining tool in sight.

Melting into the softening dusk I hope to catch sight of her in the light of the foyer but have no luck. Just an eagle-eyed doorman judging me with suspicion as I linger with intent. I need to be more careful. Loitering outside her hotel I run the risk of her discovering me. My impatience needs to be held in check. I scuttle around the corner and along a street until I find refuge from my recklessness in the calm of the courtyard of a small temple. On the left is a row of waxwork deities, though I can't be sure if the orange robed monk that sits at the end is real. I approach cautiously and realise by the fake hair line of his shaved head that it's just another of the effigies awaiting worship. Hanging around for a while, I try to soak up the solace this place seems to emanate, but my mind is blazing. I sidle past the garish monk's quarters and leave.

2

The door opened a fraction, just enough to catch my peripheral without faltering my attention. Whoever was standing half in, half out waited patiently. I stayed focused, looking ahead, watching each movement carried out in the precision I spent years to reach. I could now relax, knowing the level I'd brought them to was at its peak. It was time to pass on the baton. My brothers and sisters stood before me for a final time in salutation – open palm over fist – as I brought the class to a close. I held back the emotions, composing my professional calm and watched them leave one by one.

She made way for the trail of uniformed colours and approached me as I packed away.

'I'm sorry to bother you, but you couldn't tell me where B9 is? I'm meant to be taking a step class there.'

I tripped over my response as I glanced around, 'Um yeah, I ah, I've just finished here, I'll take you over there. It's in the next building, a bit tricky to find.'

She was stunning. A supermodel quality that was seconds from being discovered. Scandinavian features; azure eyes captivating me at once, high cheek bones, a soft wave to her long blonde hair. I asked her name as we walked the halls and down the stairs. 'Kirsten,' she said and then asked mine.

'So, Ben, what were you teaching, some sort of martial art?'

'Wing Chun Kung Fu, but it's my last day. I've handed my class over to my senior student.'

'Have you been teaching here long?'

I held open the door for her to pass through.

'About two years, a couple of nights a week. I'm finding it hard to squeeze it all in with work though.'

'Oh, what do you do?'

'I run my own design agency.' I stopped at my BMW in the car park, pressed the key and unlocked the doors, 'This is me. See the blue building on the right? Go in there and it's the first door on your left.'

'That's great, thank you. Maybe I'll see you around.'

'How about a drink to bring you up to speed on this place? Maybe later in the week.'

It wasn't like me to be so forward or have the confidence to ask someone out, but I couldn't let her go without trying. Chances are I'd never see her again.

'Oh,' she replied, her cheeks slightly reddening. 'Okay, say Thursday, here about seven?'

It was my turn to blush, 'That'd be great,' I said, and paused a second in surprise she agreed. 'Seven it is then.'

I waited in the car until seven thirty and was just about to leave when she tapped the window. She was wearing tight blue jeans and a Snoop Dogg t-shirt. I felt a little over dressed in my shirt and trousers. She lifted her finger to gesture I wait a second as she stubbed out her cigarette and got into the passenger seat as the clouds above started to seep fine rain. She slipped a mint into her mouth, 'Where are you taking me then?'

'There's a nice place just opened in Sandgate. My sister said it's already proving quite popular.'

'Manuel's?'

'That's the one, have you been?'

'Not yet. I've heard it's quite good though. Spanish place, great food by all accounts. So, are you and your sister close?'

'Yeah, we've known each other a while now,' I laughed. 'Have you got any siblings?'

She crunched her mint away, 'No, only me. I'm not much of a family person. Dad left a few years ago now and my mum is a borderline alcoholic.'

A little taken aback at the revelation, I said, 'I'm sorry to hear that. Must have been tough growing up.'

'Sometimes. I hated them arguing all the time.

When Dad finally had enough, that's when she started drinking more and more. It's got progressively worse to the point that she now hears voices in her head. She won't go to counselling, and I really don't know what to do any more.'

'I wish I could offer some advice,' I said, feeling useless in my inability to offer any help.

'It's fine, honestly. Let's not talk any more about this though.' I slipped into a space outside the restaurant and was at her door before she had a chance to open it herself. 'Chivalry's not dead after all, thanks.'

Gentle Flamenco guitar played from speakers in the background, and we were shown to our seats by a casually dressed waiter in his twenties. 'Welcome, can I get you something to drink?'

'Can you recommend any wine?' Kirsten asked as he lit a candle.

'We have a very expressive 2006 Vega Sicilia; ripe and exuberant with a beautiful herbal twist.'

'That's fine, thank you.' she replied.

'Is that red or white?' I asked, my brow raised perplexed.

Kirsten suppressed a laugh, transforming it into a warm grin, 'It's red.'

The waiter bowed ever so slightly, padded away behind the counter, and arrived back at our table bottle in hand, 'Shall I?' he asked, hovering a corkscrew.

He squeezed the cork away from the rim with a satisfying pop, holding the base of the bottle lovingly as he gently poured, quarter filling our glasses to breathe and awaited our approval. I sipped at mine trying to disguise the wince in my eyes, while Kirsten sluiced the wine around her mouth before swallowing. She nodded, 'Lovely, thank you.'

He presented us with the menus, 'I will be back with you shortly.'

'Don't you like it?' she asked as I studied the glass.

'The wine? I'm not really a fan. I'll only have half a glass as I'm driving.'

'More of a beer or spirits guy?'

'I don't drink that much. Maybe a glass of sherry at my father's insistence at Christmas, but that's about it. I just never really got the hang of it, and to be honest I don't like the taste. I got terribly drunk on Southern Comfort on my eighteenth birthday and I vowed never to do it again.'

'Not sure if I like the taste either half the time, but it curves the edge around my day.'

She drank from her glass deeply and poured another, proffered the bottle, but I declined with a raised hand and a smile.

We ordered a tapas platter to share and chatted effortlessly throughout the meal. At the best of times, I wasn't very good at the whole dating scene, but Kirsten made conversation easy, limiting any silences with questions. Instead of freezing with nerves, I found myself talking to her like she was an old friend.

'How long have you had your business? What is it you do again, design or something?'

I poured a generous glass of water. 'About three years. It's a creative agency; book and album covers, photography, graphic design; promotional material mainly, that sort of thing.'

'Anybody famous?'

'Only local stuff so far, but hopefully it's leaning towards bigger things. I worked on a couple of books for a famous author last year and I'll be doing more stuff for his publishing company later this month. I'm in talks next week with a record company that might score me a big deal.'

'Wow, that's great, I hope it goes well. So, how did you find it working at the leisure centre then?'

'Good. A few of the management can be a bunch of little Hitlers, but generally it's okay. How are you getting on there?'

'Yeah, not so bad. I know what you mean about the management. Steve Jenkins, is it? He's a bit of a one. I came in yesterday ten minutes late and he was on me like a shot quoting efficient punctuality procedures.'

'Ah, Steve. Yeah, he's a bit of an idiot. I let a class overrun a couple of months ago and he filed a report. Little man syndrome or something I guess.' I took a sip of water, 'If he gets too heavy, mention Lizzie Davies. Just say something along the lines of "I spoke to Lizzie last week and she asked after you." That should shut him up.'

'Who's Lizzie Davies?'

'Oh, only someone who nearly took him to court for sexual harassment.'

'Really?'

I chuckled, 'Yeah. He never physically did anything, but he fancied her rotten. She worked in the massage department. When he asked her out and she rejected him, he made her life a living hell. Gave her fake warnings for always being late, fabricated accusations from disgruntled customers, that sort of thing. He wouldn't leave her alone. She was left with no choice but to play dirty with him. He ended up settling out of court.'

'I knew this drink would be worth my while.'

I sported a grin, 'Not just for the gossip I hope.'

The last lights were dimming and the customers dwindling, but we were oblivious to it all. The waiter came over with our bill, a hint that his long night was desperate to end. I paid, despite her objection. 'It was my pleasure,' I said. 'I've had a lovely night.'

'Me too. Thanks, Ben.'

We leant against the car as she lit a cigarette.

She offered me the packet, 'No thanks.'

'Don't tell me, you don't smoke either.'

'Nope. Sorry to disappoint.'

'Not at all. I hope we can do this again.'

'I'd love that.'

'Lend me your phone,' she said, holding out her hand.

She swung her head to one side to avoid the spiralling smoke and typed her number into my contacts, lighting her face with dancing shadows from the screen and the orange glow from her cigarette. The sea sweeping the pebbles across the road seemed that much nearer with the dead of night. She handed it back to me, 'Give me a call.'

I was caught in the conundrum of how long to leave it; two days, three, a week? I settled with three, although I wanted to call her the next day. I could tell from her tone that she was happy to hear from me, her voice light, a smile bouncing through the airways. She agreed to meet me for a drink a few days later. There was a quiet pub not far from my house that I'd stop by every now and then for a coffee with my English Springer Spaniel, Marcus. The owners Jerry, and his wife Samantha, loved Marcus. They had a Jack Russell, and we'd often find ourselves bumping into each other while out walking along the shingle in the evenings. A few words would turn into hours of conversation by the time the sun sank into the sea. I was looking forward to Kirsten meeting them. I hoped the warm atmosphere in the bar would be enough to put her at ease.

It was well over an hour before she strolled through the doors. She came up behind me, leant in and kissed me on the cheek. 'Hey, you,' she breathed into my ear.

'Ah, you must be Kirsten,' said Samantha, holding her hand out over the bar.

Kirsten seemed unaware to the friendly extension and whispered to me that she had to use the ladies' room. I smiled at Sam sheepishly and ordered a lemonade and a glass of red wine, taking a seat at a table by the window. Kirsten returned from the toilet twitching and rubbing her nose. She came and sat beside me. I didn't have the chance to ask her about her day, she animatedly chattered, throwing questions at me about mine. I'd answer, but she'd cut in with the next question, eyes wide, brimming with energy.

'How long have you been into fitness?' I managed.

She grinned, 'Oh you're so funny, Ben. You're really trying to get to know me, that's so sweet.' With that she planted an over firm kiss on my lips, my eyes darting from side to side. She leant back, took a deep sniff, and slugged her drink back, 'Another?'

Jerry was at the bar when Kirsten approached to order. I was pleased to see they were hitting it off. She must have said something funny as Jerry roared with laughter. He tilted his head back, his hand momentarily pausing from drying a glass. He glanced over and flashed me a wink. Even Sidney, an old boy who regularly nursed the bar, was in on the joke. He knew me well, had done since I was young. He used to work as a gardener for my parents. Arthritis had got the better of his hands, leaving them gnarled and twisted. But somehow, he always managed to lift a glass of stout and roll a cigarette. He raised his tweed cap and combed back his thinning white strands as he nearly choked on his drink. 'You've got a good one here, Benny boy,' he called over. I threw him an easy familiar frown. I hated being called Benny.

I asked Kirsten what was so amusing when she came back to the table, but she just grinned and winked, 'That's for us to know.' Whatever it was, I was glad she got on so well with them.

Later we gazed in silence at the sunset on the beach behind my house and she slid her hand in mine, squeezing it tightly. I suddenly knew this was what I always wanted. Sure, I'd had schoolboy crushes, felt the heartache and pain, but what was unfolding between us felt so real, so very right. It was early days. I was fully aware of the infancy, but when you know you've got treasure in your hand, you just want to keep hold of it and never let it go.

3

My zopiclone hangover weighs heavy and unwanted while the noise of the street tears at my severed nerves. Settling into a late lunch back at the cafe opposite her hotel, I hide away from view in the corner of the shadows, knowing she'd never frequent a place such as this.

When I least expect it, there she is, laughing and joking with a guy maybe ten years older than her. He wears his money abundantly – styled jet hair, well-tailored suit, black leather brogues shining as they walk. He's relaxed with her. The confidence of someone who has little to worry about financially. He has a European look about him, Italian maybe. Her high heels clip in time to the rustle of designer bags hanging from her arms. A pang of anxiety fizzes and I bite my lip, hold my breath and count to ten. They glide into the hotel and disappear, and I'm left with only hollow thoughts of what the shopping trip has bought.

Staying close by for an hour more only makes matters worse. Wherever I am, I don't want to be. My thoughts press into my brain, giving me a stinging headache. I need to find a distraction, or I know only too well how the burden will affect me. People tend to squeeze the life out of me, but then my own company suffocates me more. The taxi driver I hail takes me to Wat Saket.

'Temple of the Golden Mount,' he says. 'Very nice.'

When we arrive, I ask him to wait outside. I like him, he says nothing to me as he drives.

I meander up the steps, caring little for the ornaments and figures that glare a story of Buddha's life. At the midway point there's a line of large dark metallic bells. Groups of tourists ring them to bring luck or possibly meaning to their lives. Stepping past, I see a gong at the end and catch the eye of one of the travellers about to take a swing. I instantly recognise her from the hotel. She holds my eye for a moment, smiles and then poses for the photo her friend has set up.

From the summit I have a panoramic view of the entire city. Stretching out for miles, dilapidated buildings squeeze in between red temple rooftops with skyscrapers framing the horizon. Sweat sticks my shirt to my back. Though the sky is pearl white with a threat of imminent rain, it's ridiculously hot. I shuffle around a golden chedi to absorb the view from all sides until my concentration is broken by laughing. The girls from the hotel have made it to the top. Before they have a chance to zone in on my position, I step behind them and descend the stairs as discreetly as possible. Halfway down I'm drawn to a standstill by a stone family gathered over a group of vultures picking away at a deceased family member. For a moment the macabre scene has me transfixed, unbalancing my resolve with what's ahead.

My phone vibrates and snaps me out of the trance. I unlock to see a text instructing me to go to an address in Chinatown at 8pm. Prickles of tension rise through my body along with disappointment that it's all come to this. Questions tighten in my throat; What am I doing? Could there be some other way? What will happen to my world once this is all over?

I ask the driver if I can hire him for the next two days. He agrees the generous deal I offer and leaves me at my hotel. The staff here are incredibly nice. I'm annoyed that I find myself reflecting a smile when I receive the wi-fi code. I wish I didn't cave in so easily to their kindness. I need to keep a hard edge, a frozen inner sanctum to do what I came here to do. Once my door is closed behind me, I expel the trapped air from my lungs and gasp, free from the suffocation the outside compresses upon me. Of people. Of the need to unnecessarily communicate any more than they must. It confirms they've banked me into their memory, etched me into their brains to call forth my face for future reference. I am now a part of them, them a part of me, however small. There's enough going on in my head without them adding to the years of stale storage I'm so desperate to escape.

My heartbeat eases, but still with a sharpness of stress that pumps the blood too fast. The room returns from monochrome to colour, swaying my consciousness, keeping my knuckles gripped to the duvet until the ice disappears and the cold sweat evaporates. I knock back a couple of diazepams with several gulps of duty-free vodka, withdraw my phone, execute Facebook, and go straight to her profile: so open and on display. A post dated yesterday shows her faking a smile with the title, 'My Man', Rodrigo from Portugal. A summary of their short existence is wrapped up in an album labelled, 'Wedding', starting with several pictures of an expensive engagement ring on her finger with the captions, 'All Set', 'Can't Wait' and one unbelievably named, 'Bling A Ding Ding'. The same pose to different backgrounds: the two united with ring on display, identical smiles for the first fifteen photos, his slightly lowering in the last five. I down some more vodka and lock my screen.

How could I have allowed this to happen? To let her leave my side. Before her, life seemed so simple. I had friends. Family. I can hear the laughter, remember the shared moments, the jokes that cleared the dark clouds on rainy days. I'm not sure what's a dream and what's real anymore. I try to grasp at what I think is a moment of clarity, but I've been so confused of late that I'm left shivering in the cold haze of fogged memories.

4

The third year of school had settled into a rainy autumn after six weeks of freedom. Nobody wanted to be here aside from the few who liked school. For me, art and photography acted as a gateway to another world, and I spent most lunchtimes in the Art and Design block in a dark room processing photographs or with my head down over gridded paper technical drawing or hands covered in ink from the print room. The first time I really noticed Danny I was working on a fictional rock band's album cover, trying to recreate the work of one my idols Roger Dean with air brushes, but I was getting more paint on the table than the square piece of card. The crash of the door coincided with Danny knocking my jam jar of water to the floor. He slid under my desk, panting, face furrowed in fear. I bent over, picked up the jar and looked at him by my feet.

He raised his finger to his lips and whispered, 'Please.'

Equally out of breath, Brett Duncan and Darren Matthews charged into the room, unbalancing the jam jar again, this time smashing into tiny pieces. I got down on all fours, gingerly picking up the fragments, blocking the view to Danny with my back.

'Where is he, Langley?' Brett growled, wiping sweat into his short, strawberry blond hair and around his face, accentuating the mass of freckles covering his skin.

'Who?' I asked as I placed the larger pieces of glass on the desk.

'You know who, the chink.'

'There's nobody here aside from me and you two. And from the look of it, you could do with spending some more time in PE.'

'Do you wanna smack in the mouth?'

'Do you? Because your teeth can join all this glass on the floor.'

He lurched towards me, but Darren held him back, 'I wouldn't do that if I were you.'

'Yeah? Why not?' Brett replied.

'I'll tell you later.'

They searched the classroom, upturning other students' work, creating chaos in their wake. I slid a four-foot canvas across the space under my desk as they turned to my position again.

Brett came so close to me I could smell his salt and vinegar breath, 'Well, if you see him, tell him we're looking for him.'

'Will do, see you then,' I smirked.

I followed them to the doorway, watching them skulk down the corridor to the main doors. They were met at the entrance by Mr Jones, the head of Art and Design.

'Ah, leaving us so soon, Mr Matthews and Mr Duncan? Not staying for some extracurricular activity?'

'No sir,' they both replied simultaneously.

'On your way then. You're letting the cold in,' Mr Jones said as he held open the door.

'Love the new threads by the way, Glynn. Suits you, sir,' Brett remarked, trying to keep a straight face.

Glancing down at his beige blazer and matching trousers, he responded, 'Hmm. And a detention suits you, Duncan. How about at the end of the day?'

'Nah, you're alright sir, but thanks anyway.'

They laughed, slamming the door behind them.

Mr Jones stopped in front of me, 'All okay in here, Ben?'

'Yep, just trying to get the hang of these old-fashioned airbrushes.'

'Ah yes, good luck with that.'

'Right, cheers, sir.'

He strolled over to his office, leaving Danny and me alone.

'They're gone now,' I said, moving the canvas away. I leant forward and peered under the table.

Danny was crouched tightly in the corner.

He looked over, expelling a drawn-out breath, 'You sure?'

I put my hand out and helped him to his feet. He brushed himself down. 'What's got you into their bad books then?'

'Living, breathing, generally day to day existing.'

He sat down at my desk and stared at my work.

'You shouldn't let them push you around like that. If you don't stand up to them, they'll always give you a hard time.'

'Have you seen the size of them? Two years they've been giving me crap. Everyday I've had to give them my lunch money for protection, but they've doubled the price. New term tax they called it, and I didn't have it.'

There was something about Danny I instantly warmed to. He had an uncanny likeness to a young Bruce Lee which was a great start with me.

'Do you like Kung Fu?' I asked.

'Why, because I'm Asian? We don't all practice Kung Fu so drop the stereotyping!'

'Sorry. I'm Ben.' I put my hand across the table.

He shook it, 'I wish I did do Kung Fu. I'd get a lot less hassle from those two. That was brave of you though, to front them like that.'

'A little bravery and stupidity can go a long way, mate. Darren tried the protection money thing with me on the first day of school. Notice the chipped tooth on his bottom set?'

'Yeah.'

'Moi.'

His eyes widened along with a grin.

'What are you up to after school?' I asked as I pulled out a squashed cheese and crisp sandwich from my rucksack.

'Besides homework? Not much, why?'

'Do you fancy coming over to mine? My dad lets me use the garage to train in.'

'Train?' he asked, eyebrow cocked.

'Jeet Kune Do and Wing Chun.'

He paused for a moment, contemplating something behind his eyes, 'Yeah, I guess. If I can make it out of the gates that is.'

I wasn't sure if he would show. I'd train as usual, and if he came, he came. My dad always said, "Don't expect anything in life, that way if anything good happens, it's a bonus." It was about 7.20 when I heard a meek knock at the garage door. Danny stood soaked through in the evening rain, looking thoroughly miserable.

'Come in, mate. It looks bloody horrible out there.' I pulled the door down behind him a fraction. 'Hang your jacket on the wall,' I said, pointing to a hook in the corner. He wore black trainers, black trousers, black jacket, and a baseball cap. He took off his jacket to reveal a black t-shirt. He certainly looked the part, like some sort of hip-hop ninja assassin.

'Can you do Bruce's one-inch punch?' he asked, standing opposite me.

I laughed, 'Yeah.'

'Go on then.'

'Okay, if you're sure.' I walked over to my kit bag and removed a focus mitt. 'Hold this to your chest... tightly.' He did as I said. 'I won't hit at full power, just a little, so you get the idea.'

'Yeah, cool.' His eyes lit with fascination, intrigued to see if I could really do it.

I lined up my fist with the pad, a half inch away. And tapped. He stumbled backwards and crashed into a stack of tyres.

I reached over and gave him my hand. 'Are you okay?'

'Whoa! That was incredible. You hardly moved.'

'I'm not as good as I'd like to be, but I'm better than most people think I am.'

He stood, looked me up and down, awestruck. 'Can you show me how to do that?'

'If you like. But one step at a time. We'll start with the first Wing Chun form, Siu Nim Tau. This will give you all the tools you need to begin with.'

'Where did you learn all of this?'

'My uncle Tommy. He came back from Hong Kong after about twenty-five years working for a bank. All his spare time was dedicated to practising Wing Chun out there. He learnt from three Grandmasters: Wong Shun Leung, Chu Shong Tin and Ip Chun. He's awesome!'

'And he taught you?'

'Pretty much everything he knows twice a week ever since I was seven.'

'Wow, you're really lucky.'

'Yeah, I guess. It's hard though, he's quite strict.'

'Yeah, my dad's strict, never lets up.'

'Oh really?'

Danny's eyes dipped for a moment, 'My mum went back to Thailand when I was ten and never came home again, so it's just me and my dad now. He took it badly.'

'I'm sorry to hear that.'

'Thanks. Anyway, this Nimmy Tay thing?'

'Siu Nim Tau. It means, Little Idea Form.'

That first evening turned into many more, training in the garage. Danny was as good for me as I was for him. We were inseparable. Sometimes we'd watch martial arts films at my house; Jean-Claude Van Damme, Jet Li and Bruce Lee to name a few. Sometimes I'd go over to his place and learn how to play football. The kid was a genius with a ball. I was puzzled why he didn't play for the school team, but as time went on, I noticed he suffered from an acute shyness and was often withdrawn. He told me he didn't like too many people around him. I could have only put this down to the bullying he'd experienced, which made me sad thinking of all that lost potential. He'd really taken some hard knocks in life.

His dad liked to throw his weight around, let it be known Danny was living in his house and had to play by his rules. We'd play console games in his bedroom and sometimes he would burst in, as if he knew we were at a crucial part of the game, and switch everything off and order me home and Danny to his household chores. I'd often notice bruising on Danny's body that I wasn't entirely convinced was solely a result of Brett and Darren.

Danny was hooked on video games. Most evenings before we met, he retreated to his room with his curtains closed in front of a TV set. I guess that was his form of escape. My dad wouldn't let me have a console, which I didn't mind too much. He wanted me to focus on my fitness and schoolwork. My passion for drawing and photography was paramount and he didn't want anything to distract me. He didn't have a problem with me playing them at Danny's though. Luckily, his dad took a shine to me. I was always polite and accommodating to the house rules, and I often brought round meals my mum had cooked and sent with me for the two of them to heat up, which despite his father's pride, was greatly appreciated as Danny's dad couldn't cook to save his life. Danny's mum's departure took its toll on them both, especially his dad who desperately looked for the answers in the bottom of a bottle. Danny rarely spoke about his relationship with his father. It was a sore point. I did my best to respect that he had his own way of dealing with things. But it was hard watching him work with it by himself at times. I wanted to intervene somehow and take him away from it all. But as he pointed out, Danny was all his dad had left in the world.

Conversely, my family were tight, and although we had our ups and downs, we managed each day as a team. On the off chance I had an argument with my parents or sister, or schoolwork was getting me down, Danny was always there, listening intently, not judging, but giving sensible advice on how to deal with situations. He was usually right too. Older than his years, he was the kindest and funniest person I'd ever met, and generous to a fault, which is why I could see him being taken advantage of sometimes.

Uncle Tommy allowed Danny to join in on the Wing Chun lessons. We trained diligently and slowly Danny's confidence grew. So much so, that when we were leaving school one day and walking towards the bus stop, he stood up to Brett and Darren without a second thought. It was heading towards the end of the fourth year of school and although Brett and Darren had let up a bit, they still had it in for him. They shouldered him whenever they could, slurred racist remarks on the sly and generally gave him a rough time. He'd had enough.

Brett crept up behind us and pushed Danny to the ground. Danny flew into a rage. He launched at Brett, punching, and kicking him. I'd only seen this kind of speed in the movies. Darren tried to step in, but I grabbed hold of his arm, 'Unless you want me to deal with, I suggest you leave them to it.'

We stood back until I saw that Brett had had enough, cowering into a ball as Danny furiously focused all the years of pent-up aggression into him. It was hard to pull him away. He was sweating and panting, aggression burning in his eyes. By now a crowd was gathering and the last thing I wanted was for Danny to get into any trouble.

'Darren, get Brett up and out of here. Say nothing to anyone. We don't want to see you again, you hear?'

He nodded, dumbfounded at what had just happened. He hoisted Brett up, who was heavily bruised around his face, bleeding from the top of his eye and corner of his mouth and steadied him as he limped along out of site. We both made haste, walked around the corner into the park and sat on a bench as Danny gathered himself together.

'Bloody hell, are you okay?' I asked, taking a carton of Ribena from my bag, and passing it to him.

He pierced the foil with the straw and started sipping. The skin on his knuckles had split and were weeping. 'I think so. Sorry, I don't know what came over me.'

'Mate, you've no need to apologise to me. That was long overdue. If you hadn't done it, I think I would have sooner or later. You need to reign that temper in a bit though. If I wasn't around, I hate to think how far it could have gone.'

'Yeah, I know. I just couldn't stop once I started. I've taken too much from those two.'

I put my arm around him, 'Don't worry about it now, eh? Let's get you home without your dad seeing those hands. If he does, just say you scraped them on the floor of my garage when we were training or something.'

With his ever-rising confidence after the fight with Brett, Danny got a name for himself and became ever popular with some of the girls from the school nearby. He started dating a girl named Cassie, who was gorgeous with shoulder length brown hair, hazel eyes that I couldn't look at for longer than a second for fear my heart would melt, and a smile to die for. He had a real knack with the ladies, while I was utterly hopeless.

'You're too soft, mate,' he would laugh. 'You can't go in there with all hearts and flowers. Ease off and let them do the chasing a bit.'

I did tend to fall head over heels from the word go.

On his sixteenth birthday Danny invited Cassie and me to McDonald's. We arrived together with no sign of Danny. He had recently taken up weight training and had been obsessed with running before and after school. I assumed that's why he was a little late. Finally, he showed up, stood at the counter, ordered, and came over with a stacked tray with a cashier behind him holding another.

'Dig in guys,' Danny said as the trays were placed down before us. I had a face full of a Big Mac when he followed up with, 'I've applied to the Royal Marines and have been accepted. I start the PRMC next month.'

Cassie's face dropped, as did mine.

'Are you serious?' I asked, wiping my hands on a serviette.

'Yep, never more so. I got through the interview,

medical and pre-fitness and I'm all set.'

'What? And you never thought to tell me about this?' Cassie said. She looked deeply hurt, as if her whole world had come crashing down around her.

'I'm telling you now.'

She got up. 'Thanks for nothing,' she said as tears appeared, and walked out.

'You better go after her, mate.' I looked over as she went through the doors.

'Na, she'll be alright. I'll let her calm down and talk to her later.'

I still couldn't believe it. He never showed the slightest interest in the armed forces before.

'What's brought all this on?' I asked.

'Been thinking about it for a while. If I'd told you guys, you would have tried to talk me out of it, so I just went ahead and did it. My dad's been getting really bad, Ben. He's been drinking more and more and taking it out on me. I've just had enough.'

I couldn't blame him. Although he was loyal to his father, there were times I thought things were going from bad to worse. Only a couple of weeks ago he turned up to school sporting a black eye and was cagey about it. I knew it had something to do with his father. God knows how he kept so upbeat about it all, but I guess that was his way of handling things.

Cassie and Danny were no more after that night. Despite his reassurances, she wasn't having any of it. The fact that he'd gone behind her back was enough to seal the deal. I called round to see him just as she was leaving. 'You're welcome to him,' she said, storming out.

I went upstairs into his room. Danny was sitting with a can of Budweiser on the table, console controller in hand as if nothing had happened.

'You alright mate?' I asked, sitting on the bed next to him.

'Yes mate, couldn't be better. Women, eh?'

'She looks pretty upset.'

'She'll get over it.'

And that was that. A month later he called me after four days training on the Potential Royal Marines Course in Lympstone. 'I'm in,' he shouted down the phone elated.

'Wow! That's fantastic, Danny, congratulations. But hey, anybody could do it. Piss easy, yeah?'

'You kidding me?'

I laughed. 'How did it go? What was the course like?'

His enthusiasm was at a peak, 'Ah mate, it was crazy, pure evil. I was sick three times. We did all sorts of stuff: excruciating runs with full kit, gym tests, you know, pull ups, sit ups, press ups and swim tests, and bastard obstacle and assault courses. I'm totally knackered. I've got bruises and blisters all over. I'll tell you more and show you some pictures soon.'

'I'm well made up for you. What now?'

'I have to decide if I want to continue on to the thirty-two-week basic training course at the commando training centre in Lympstone.'

'And will you?'

'Yes mate, can't wait.'

My heart dropped. Up until now it was a fantasy in my head, but it suddenly became very real. I was about to lose my best friend to Her Majesty.

5

In the back alleys of Chinatown, I slog heavy-headed through the crush of shoppers eyeing stalls of fish on ice, rows of flattened red roasted ducks dangling from coat hangers and hooked carcases of pigs; flies feeding and laying eggs around their eyes. I bypass a beggar, an empty cup waiting desperately for coins before his bony lifeless legs. He raises the stumps of his leprosy-infected wrists and deplores with his watery eyes for me to donate.

In the courtyard of a small Chinese temple, I look around for a sign of an office or doorway. A young boy rides a bike to my position and gawps up at me in fascination. I look past him at the elaborate dragons encircling the temple columns in hope he'll move on. When the relentless stare all but grinds me down, he's saved from the words about to escape my mouth by Danny appearing from a shaded corner, beckoning me in silence to follow. He says nothing at first but gestures for me to take a seat at a desk in a room, bare but for a lightbulb and a stand-alone fan. He sits opposite and opens a drawer, pulls out a half bottle of whiskey, two glasses and a packet of cigarettes. He pours the honey-coloured liquid to half fill the glasses, takes a cigarette from the packet, and slides the box across to me. I light one, exhale the smoke and take a sip of the Mekhong whiskey, wincing at the sour-sharp burning in my throat. He smiles a familiar, almost comforting smile and I realise how much I've missed him. He flicks his ash to the floor and leans forward, a slight frown weighing his brow, 'It's been a while, Ben, how are you?'

'I've been better,' I reply, leaning back as the numbness of alcohol saturates me.

He sniggers, 'You look rubbish, mate. Is there a Charles Manson lookalike contest on in Thailand?'

I rub my beard, pull back my hair, 'Thanks. You don't look so bad yourself.'

'How do you like Bangkok?'

'I'd like to leave.'

'I'm not sure you're cut out for all of this you know.' I go to speak, but he interrupts before I have the chance, 'About our plan...'

I stand to pull my wallet out, but he puts up a hand and tells me to sit, 'I don't want a penny from you, Ben. I'll sort things out like I said, but it's going to take time.'

'What? I thought...'

'I think that's half of your problems, you think too much. You need to stay calm. I'll let you know when the time's right, but for now, drink and take it easy.'

He removes his baseball cap and rubs the bristles of his cropped hair and massages the base of his thick neck. He knows me well enough to recognise when I'm jittery and I wonder if he can spot it now.

'She's still in Bangkok.'

He empties his glass and tops mine up until I tell him to stop.

'I know. I've been keeping an eye on her comings and goings on social media. She's got no idea I'm here.'

'Good. Keep it that way. Tomorrow morning, she flies to Chiang Mai.'

I frown, 'How do you know her movements so well?'

'It doesn't matter how I know, but I do. Wipe the doubt off your face, Ben. You can trust me. Anyway, I've got you a plane ticket.' He opens the drawer and takes out an envelope, 'Here.'

My shoulders drop, 'I'm sorry. Everything's got me so paranoid.'

'That's what I worry about.' He stands, dragging his chair behind him, the cue for me to leave. I down the whiskey, nearly bringing it back up again. 'Keep safe, Ben.'

The streets are alight with neon signage, the pavements awash with locals and tourists. My cab is waiting, the driver snoozing behind the wheel until I open the door and get in. I ask to be taken to the Grand Palace, one of the most popular tourist attractions in Thailand, with the intention of taking a long walk from there back to the hotel. I hope it will clear the fog of booze and the barrage of thoughts racing for my attention.

For some reason the complex is on lock-down and I am checked by security before I enter the road that passes the palace. The officer looks me up and down then ushers me through. High castellated white walls hide all but the golds and reds of the illuminated roof tiers and gables. Edgy armed guards stand watch by a set of gleaming ornamental elephants centred in the road to serve as a roundabout. When the lights of the palace are all faded and I'm on a quiet street, I stop for a moment, try to collect myself before moving on. There are too many voices in my head – hers, mine, Danny's, others I can't name, infinite crowds competing against each other. Everything is a slur of the past flowing through me. I shake my head, mutter for them to stop, but they only increase as I walk on.

Eventually I arrive in a street littered with food carts, wafting kerosene, and unhygienic ingredients for the masses that horde them. People sit at tables or on kerbs picking at what's on offer. I glance at a man who catches my attention with his ladle as he stirs a foul looking stew of animal innards in gravy. 'You wanna try?' he says, grinning and exposing his toothless gums. I ignore him and walk further on to a KFC and explore some bones for fragments of chicken.

By the time I reach the hotel, I'm beat. I collapse on the bed, eager for sleep. Moments later I'm disturbed by a commotion of voices and banging outside. I open my door to see what's going on and find the two girls, clearly drunk.

'Do you mind? Some of us are trying to sleep,' I bark.

'Sorry, we had a bit of late night. We're leaving tomorrow, so we'll be out of your hair,' says the prettier one. She smiles gently and puts out her hand as she introduces herself. 'Amy, by the way.' I turn my back and slam the door.

The commotion continues, only louder and more deliberate. My teeth chatter, my hands shake. I reach into my luggage and take out the bottle of vodka, take a large swig to wash down two pills and sit back, waiting for the night to absorb me.

6

Heavy rain lashed at the house and the wind was ripping up the tide. I was sitting alone, working against the clock on a project for Panik Records. It was just after midnight when a loud knock set Marcus off barking into the darkness of the hall. I tore my eyes away from my laptop and unlocked the door to find Kirsten drenched, mascara running down her cheeks where she'd been crying. She told me her landlord had tried to evict her and when she had resisted, he'd turned violent, pushing her around the apartment. Despite my insistence, she didn't want to involve the police and we spent the best part of the night discussing the prospect of her living with me. It made sense as she was nearly always at my house anyway. I offered to help her collect the rest of her things the next morning, but she asserted she would take care of it herself.

Now we were an official couple, I hoped Kirsten would connect with my family. I had always been close to my sister, Louise, and as there wasn't much of an age gap, I was sure her and Kirsten could become friends. I arranged several dinners, but each time she cancelled at the last-minute citing work pressures. I couldn't blame her. It must be difficult to engage in a new family, especially when you're not used to having much of one yourself. I managed to pin Kirsten down for my parents' 40th wedding anniversary. It was a small affair. Dinner and drinks at a local restaurant. She played the part well enough and seemed to get on particularly well with Louise's husband, Greg. He was a finance hotshot, something to do with mergers and acquisitions in London.

When we got home, Kirsten admitted that she'd felt uncomfortable throughout dinner.

'I don't think your Mum and Dad like me,' she said.

'Of course they like you. They've just not had much of a chance to get to know you until tonight.'

I wasn't sure where this was coming from. They couldn't have been more accommodating. She said as much about Louise too and asked me why she kept giving her funny looks.

'Funny looks? How?' I asked.

'I don't think she liked me talking to Greg. Maybe she was jealous, but it wasn't my fault he kept making a beeline for me. Even offered to take me out in his Aston Martin.'

'That was nice of him, but honestly, I don't think you have anything to worry about. Louise is happy for us.'

'If you say so. But still, I don't think I'll go to any more of your family gatherings. It's bad enough Danny hangs around all the time, without the added pressure of any more of the Ben clan.'

'What's Danny got to do with it?'

'I think he's a drain on the business and an unnecessary expense.'

'Really? He's helping the business grow; getting new clients onboard. We'd be lost without him.'

Danny had started working for me after he returned from the armed forces. He needed a new focus, and I was grateful to have someone share the load. It was a complete gear shift for him, but one he adapted to well. I admired his ability to adopt to his new career with such positivity and dedication.

'Look, you're a trusting guy, Ben, and always think the best of people. That's one of the things I love about you, but you know as well as I do that sometimes that prevents you from seeing things as they really are. Do you really need Danny, or if you worked a little harder could you do just as well on your own? You must consider that you don't owe him anything and his wages could be money back in our bank account.'

I was dumbfounded by Kirsten's assessment, and I put it down to her being tired. The evening had probably been quite overwhelming for her, and I was sure everything would settle itself by the morning.

On the contrary, with each new day the harmony we had shared slowly dissipated. Kirsten became detached, erratic, and confrontational. Almost overnight she had embarked on a mission to find ways to push my buttons. If a window was left open it would be too cold, if I closed it, it was too hot. If I switched off a light because the room wasn't in use, she'd turn on every light in the house. If I put a bag of shopping on the floor, she would freak out and insist the entire contents be thrown away. Nothing ever seemed good enough.

In a bid to break the cycle, I suggested a holiday for us both. She was excited by the idea and arranged it the next day.

'I've booked us a week away in Tenerife,' she said. 'We've got a lovely hotel with an amazing view overlooking the sea.'

'That's great. When?'

'In a month, if you can arrange some time off.'

'That shouldn't be a problem.'

We were based just outside the beach resort of Playa de las Americas. She had chosen this location as she'd been a couple of years ago with her friend Caron. We hired a car, taking day trips out, soaking up all the island had to offer. We walked hand in hand along the cobblestone streets breathing in the flower-filled plazas and eyeing up the Castilian mansions of La Orotava, finishing with a cable-car ride at sunset to stare out at the stunning silhouette of Mount Teide. We hiked through the Teno Rural Park's laurel forests on the Agua Mountain and relaxed in the sleepy atmosphere of La Laguna Old Town with its colonial architecture and neo classical churches, taking advantage of the colourful tapas bars.

On the fourth night, over a late dinner at our hotel, Kirsten became argumentative. Everything had been going so well, but it was like a switch had flicked inside her. I carefully probed to try and understand where her head was at.

'Well, if you must know I'm finding the endless sightseeing a bit tedious. Last time I came here, it was more exciting than this.'

'What was so different, apart from who you were here with?' I asked.

'Caron knew how to have fun for a start.'

'Okay. Sorry, I thought we were having fun.'

'Really, Ben? Let's face it, it's not exactly your strong point, is it? Kirsten sat back in her chair; her arms crossed.

'What can I do to make things better? We only have a couple of days left. Let's not waste them.'

'Honestly, I don't think there's anything you can do. You are who you are and that's that.' She got up and went to leave, 'I'm going to bed.'

The following morning, she was up early and said she wanted to go out for a walk on her own, go to the beach and enjoy a bit of "me time" as she put it. As disappointed as I was, I didn't argue and let her go. I wanted her to be happy and maybe a bit of time alone to collect her thoughts would be good. I hadn't checked my emails since our arrival so I could do that and occupy myself for a couple of hours.

It was early evening when she returned. She was upbeat and despite my concern and upset at her being away for the whole day, I was pleased to see her in a good mood.

'So, what did you get up to?' I asked.

'I caught up with an old friend and well, time ran away. You know how it is,' she replied.

'Strange you should bump into someone you know this far from home.'

'Not that strange, given he lives here.'

'He?'

'I told you about Mateo. We met last year. He's a lifeguard on the beach.' This was news to me, and my mind was racing. Before I could respond, she added, 'It's so funny, he was desperate to have a threesome with Caron and me, but I wasn't really into that at the time.'

I didn't know what to say. Was she admitting to something happening between her and Mateo today? No, she hadn't said that. They probably just had a drink together. She wouldn't come back and be so relaxed about it if something had happened. Would she? Something about her nonchalance made me uneasy.

I pushed back any distrust for the sake of keeping the peace, 'Well, I'm glad you had a nice day.'

Hopes of a fresh start when we got home were short

lived. I moulded more of my time around her, delegating some of the work to my staff for a while so I could be at home more often. But it didn't make any difference. Quite the opposite. Kirsten spent more time out and even stayed away for days on end without any explanation of where she was.

One afternoon, I came home early to find her crying in the living room. 'Oh, thank God you're here. It's Marcus, I don't know what to do.'

Marcus was laying by the back doors, his tongue hanging limply to one side. He didn't respond as I came in like he normally would, and I noticed white froth foaming around his mouth.

'Kirsten, what's happened?' I asked as I rushed to his side to see what was wrong.

'I don't know, he was like that when I got home.'

'Have you called the vet?'

'No, I thought I should wait for you.'

'What? Why? Clearly, he needs help.'

I couldn't believe what I was hearing, but my priority right now was Marcus. I rushed him straight to the vet, but it was too late. He had ingested poison and the toxicity was too great for him to fight it. Devastated, I returned home to an empty house. There was no sign of Kirsten and when I tried calling her all I got was her voicemail. I sat alone and couldn't stop crying.

Around 10pm Kirsten came home. She was laughing on her mobile and cut the call short when she saw me. 'How's the dog?'

'Marcus was put to sleep this afternoon.

Apparently, he ingested poison.'

'It must have been the neighbours.'

'What are you talking about?'

'Poisoned meat, something like that. Happens all the time.'

'No, it doesn't. Why would you say that?'

'So, what, you're saying I did it?'

'Of course not.'

'It sounds like it to me. You always put that dog before me. Sometimes it feels like you don't care about me at all.'

'You're my world.'

'I probably am now the dog's gone. Maybe now you'll find time for me in your busy schedule.'

'That's so unfair, Kirsten. You know that's not true; I always have time for you.'

'I'm only telling you how I feel. I love you, Ben, but you make me feel like I'm not important to you. I'm just saying the silver lining in all this is that now you might have a bit more time for us. One less distraction, you know.'

Inside I was beside myself with grief, but I knew it was a weight I'd have to bear alone. I couldn't risk losing Kirsten as well and had to prove to her she was my number one priority.

7

A burning sensation consumes my body and panic sends me to a cold shower where I do all I can to hold myself together and stop myself from throwing up. I close the door quietly as I leave and find my driver sitting on his bonnet, head up worshipping the sun. He takes his sunglasses from his shirt pocket, slips them on and opens the back door for me to slide in. His scrawny frame sits before me and he adjusts the interior mirror, 'Good morning, where I take you?'

'Somewhere for breakfast,' I reply, settling into the seat.

He hasn't driven for long before we come to a smart hotel. Inside, the smells of freshly baked bread, muffins, and fried food seep into the foyer. I order eggs and bacon, coffee and toast and unlock my phone. Facebook shows she's checked into

Chiang Mai International Airport just as Danny had said. My breakfast arrives and I do my best to work through it, drinking more coffee than eating. The sun burns the back of my neck through the window, making my headache intolerable. I slip a couple of paracetamols down with a bottle of water and head back to the cab.

The day is mine. I have nothing to do but wait. I lay myself on the line with my driver, hoping I can trust him. 'Ananada, where can I get some dope?'

'Dope, sir?' he replies, glancing in the mirror.

I mime a deep toke of a joint with my fingers, 'You know, grass, hashish?'

'Oh, I am not sure.'

'Will a thousand baht make you think clearer?'

'No need for money. I take you to place called Koh San Road. Here you find many thing. But please, be careful. Police station is at end of road and area is often patrolled.'

'Thanks, I will be.'

He drops me at the top of a street infested with hippy backpackers hugging shop fronts covered in tie-dye clothing, cheap slogan t-shirts, cafes, and hotels by the plenty. Ananada tells me to call him on his mobile when I need him again and I slide out into the blistering heat.

This is far from my kind of place. Too noisy and intense. Hawkers grope at me trying to sell tacky souvenirs that I can't see anybody wanting to buy. I take refuge in a dingy cafe, wrestle my heartburn with some indigestion tablets and order a beer, hoping I can spot anybody that looks remotely stoned. I don't have to wait long. By the time I start my second bottle, two guys in their mid-twenties roll in reeking of weed. One has an old scar along the base of his neck as if he's had his throat cut. The other, who ties his dreadlocks back as he sits near me, looks over and says, 'You alright mate?' after noticing I'm staring at them. I nod, drag on my cigarette, and look over the road to a couple of overweight English guys on the wrong side of fifty trying to chat up a Thai girl in her early teens.

I get up and sit down next to Dread. The audacity of my approach pains his face, but I stop him before he has time to react.

'I need to get some weed.'

'Yeah and?' Scar says in heavy Scouse.

'Can you help me out?'

'Yeah, turn around and piss off.'

'Let's not be like that hey?' I slide a thousand baht across the table. 'For your trouble lads, and whatever I have to pay for the gear.'

'What, you the tourist police or somint?' asks Dread.

'Do I look Thai?'

'Mate, you don't have to be. Plain clothes British bizzies work alongside the Thais.'

'I'll bear that in mind. Look, I just want a smoke that's all.'

Scar pauses, looks me straight in the eye. I hold the stare until he relents, 'How much do you need?'

'A quarter?'

'Go back to your table, finish your bevvy and we'll come and see you in a minute.'

'Thanks.' I do as he says without looking back.

Ten minutes later they tap me on the shoulder and nod for me to follow. We walk halfway up the road, down an alley and into a cheap guest house that nearly chokes me in a thick cloud of patchouli incense. At the top of the stairs, they unlock the door to their room and motion me inside.

Scar lurks behind me as Dread rifles through his backpack. He pulls out two lead containers, 'Polly or bud?'

'Huh?'

'Pollen or grass, brown or green?'

'Oh, solids I guess, less smell.'

He puts a box back and undoes the other to reveal a large bar of shiny brown dope. Scar comes around to face me, a little too close for comfort, while Dread removes a set of scales and warms a knife, cuts, and weighs.

'How much?' I ask as he hands it to me.

'How much have you got?'

'Enough.'

'Enough it is then.' They look at each other and smirk.

I pull out my wallet, open it and Scar withdraws all my notes, amounting to nearly ten thousand baht.

'Oh, I see,' I say calmly, not expecting I was here to be robbed.

'Get lost then,' Scar says as he pockets the

money.

I unleash a palm strike straight at his mouth which connects with a satisfying crunch. He stumbles back, spitting fragments of his bloodied upper teeth. I rush forward and throw all my weight into his temple with my elbow. He lands heavily, murmurs something and passes out on one of the beds. Dread stands still, unsure of what to do next. He steps forward to reach for the knife on the bureau, but I catch him with a hard kick to his kneecap. He crumples to the floor screaming.

'Are you stupid or what? Do you think I go around asking people for gear like some sort of idiot who can't look after himself?' I stamp on Dread's knee and grind my foot into the bone. He lets out a pitiful scream as I lean into his face. I put my finger to my lips, 'Shhh, there's a good boy.'

Taking my money and all their brown, I leave, closing the door behind me. I pace to the end of the road, past the police station and around the corner to a Burger King. I order a strawberry milkshake and saunter into the toilet. In the cubicle, I put down the toilet seat, take out a cigarette, empty the tobacco, mix half of it with some of the hash and then re-stuff the contents and go outside into the fresh air to light up.

It hits me instantly, accompanying the soft cushion of beer I'd drunk earlier. Right now, all I want is to be wasted in my room, but I know only too well the repercussions of being alone with the carnival of mirrors that promise to drive me mad.

Instead, I hail a tuk tuk to take me somewhere. Anywhere. Fifteen minutes later we arrive at the Temple of the Reclining Buddha, Wat Pho. It looks busy from the outside, tourists and worshippers entering and exiting. I find a small lane nearby to make another joint. A scrawny black kitten toys with a dead mouse at my feet as I smoke.

I start to relax, the stress of the last few days unloading from my shoulders as I take my time and stroll around the complex of colossal colourful chedis. It's only when I step into the hall of the huge golden reclining Buddha that I feel the need to exit as soon as possible. The place is packed with tourists taking pictures, clogging the narrow hallway without any spatial awareness. The heat adds to the claustrophobia and the tension builds up by the time I'm spat out of the other end.

Finding a degree of peace in a coffee shop close by, I open my phone. On Instagram, posted in the last hour, is a picture of the happy couple at an expensive villa with a large swimming pool and hills beyond. The title beneath reads, 'Our lovely home for the next week.' Familiar voices swim into my head and turn my gut; hatred, betrayal and anger, a bed of heartbreak resting beneath. I slam my cup down and hold my head in both hands. It's time I went back to the hotel.

The walls of my room close around me, the hash and vodka beckoning for release. The voices flow in and out until the fourth glass, the fourth joint and the fourth pill board me onto a train of sleep.

Before I have a chance to register the banging at the door, it's flung open. I'm dragged to the floor, my spine kneaded hard by somebody's foot. I yell out incoherently but find no answers. If I do, they're returned in a squabble of Thai. I'm yanked up, thrown against the wall to come face to face with a peaked cap cop, spraying broken English into my face. I'm lost to the confusion, unable to decipher the sudden chaos unfolding.

I'm hauled into a van with barred windows holding handcuffed locals sat side by side, staring down at their shackled feet and awaiting whatever fate decides for them. In a large hall I line up in one of the many rows, forced to strip naked and squat as I'm checked for what I can only assume is smuggled contraband. I try to plead, try to make sense, but I am screamed at by a guard and told to keep quiet, flung a pair of knee length shorts and herded into a hallway where my photograph is taken against a height chart. My head is shaved, I'm given a rolled blanket and I enter a yard to the shouting and jeering of a thousand tattooed faces.

I can't take the pushing and shoving, and I explode, punching and clawing for air. I hit out, connecting with someone's face. The anger wills me on and I hit someone else. I'm pulled away, wrestling clutching arms, this new world a bloody blur wherever I look. I'm suddenly hit from behind and lose consciousness.

When I awake curled and frightened, I'm

disorientated by the early bleaching sun igniting my skin through a barred window. I lay cramped with maybe thirty or forty men, the overwhelming reek of urine, sweat and faeces smothering my senses. The squalid cell is all but quiet aside from a few snores and shuffling bodies trying to find comfort on the stone floor.

I stare out and watch the sun rise higher and witness others awake to a guard's morning call. Again, I'm shoved around by other inmates, jostling for my attention. I can't understand a word, but I don't give them the satisfaction of my burst patience. Instead, I find a corner of the cell in the hope I'm left alone, but my peripheral is disturbed by heroin addicts chasing the dragon from slithers of foil as cockroaches crawl over their toes. I turn away in desperate hope of a shred of serenity, but my eyes are cast to a fellow prisoner as he screams in fear as he's violated by another inmate, four others in line awaiting their turn. In the distance a strangulated pipe tune bleats, muffled by the yelling of a crowd coaxing a brutal confrontation between two men. One is handed a makeshift shank and plunges it into the stomach of his foe. A guard runs a baton along the barred windows, stops and focuses his smile directly at me. He pulls a gun, points it at my face and pulls the trigger.

Saturated in sweat and gasping for breath I feel the air-conditioning chill on my skin. The room is in darkness, the faint noise of traffic a million miles away. I groan as I lift my head from the pillow, right myself slowly and make my way out into the thickness of the warm evening air, the dream still haunting me. Walking under the flyovers, past the disregarded homeless and trash swept away from the immediate eyeline, I haven't a clue where I'm heading. Trawling the streets with the ever-pressing sounds of car horns and drunk travellers shouting from rickshaws, I near a quiet edge of the Chao Phraya River with only the sound of rippling water and the motors of boats and ferries passing by – a treasured respite from the continuous garble in my head. I stare out at the trails of high rises, lights from their tiny windows blurring in my vision.

My mind drifts back to those long summer days, stretched out with the scent of a sea breeze, the two of us hand in hand gliding along the seafront. Nothing mattered then, we had the whole world ahead of us; warm memories at our backs gently pushing us along. The only two people on earth, laughing, chasing the clouds home. If only she could step back into my world; restore the joy and the laughter we shared.

A message alert breaks the solace, the stinging light of my phone display reads, 'Make sure you're on that flight... Danny.' I sense his doubt in my resolve to see this through, and as I look at my feet hovering above the midnight of the water, the pull to sink below becomes so strong.

8

Arguments were common and my back was breaking trying to heave the weight. I began responding to Kirsten's erratic outbursts in kind. I knew it was futile to entertain such confrontation, but the rational side of me was beyond reach. Work suffered because of my lack of focus and attention being elsewhere. I constantly forgot meetings and made mistakes. Danny implored me to take some time out, for my sake as well as the business. Neither were heading in a good direction and Danny knew all too well how easy it was to get stuck on a dark path.

When Danny first returned to Kent, I had no idea he was back. Since being up for selection into the Special Boat Service, contact between us became infrequent, to put it mildly. I'd received a scrawled note a few months earlier, just to let me know he was still alive. Other than that, I had no idea where he was or what he was up to. He was busy fulfilling his dream, as was I.

One evening I came home late from a new client meeting and saw a dishevelled guy hanging around my front door. He had scruffy hair, a few weeks stubble and wore a dirty white tracksuit. I approached with caution.

'Danny?' I enquired.

'Alright Ben.'

'Bloody hell, mate. I almost didn't recognise you. Are you coming in?'

It felt like that first night when we were kids in the garage all over again, hardly knowing him, unsure what to expect or say. I put the kettle on and asked how he was, what he'd been up to, but he remained aloof.

'Danny, say something, mate. I haven't seen or heard from you for ages.'

'I don't know what to say. Don't ask me about the regiment. I don't want to talk about it. I'm just glad to be home.'

Beyond his eyes, he was a completely different person. The fresh-faced, enthusiastic young man that left to pursue a tough, yet exciting career as a soldier was not the person before me now. He looked weary and lost, but more than that there was a calmness about him that was oddly unnerving, almost deadly. He sat rigid with a wild stare, and I became quite unnerved that at any moment he was going to snap, and all hell would break loose.

We sat in an awkward silence. He drank his cup of tea and got up to leave.

'Stay if you want,' I offered, but he made his excuses and headed to the door.

Little by little over the course of several weeks he started to open up, relaxing more in my company. I gave him all the time he needed to settle back into his new life that he seemed so unsure of. It was as if he was stranded in no man's land, a desolate area between his time in the forces and this foreign field he once called home.

'My mate Mackey and me were in Afghan,' he blurted out one afternoon as we were staring out to sea from my living room window. 'We'd been instructed to detonate a pile of explosives in a tunnel used by the Taliban. I went in and set up all the charges, came out and we waited but nothing happened. We hung around for another forty minutes just in case. I was about to go back in when Mackey said that he'd go instead; told me to get the vehicle ready. He laughed and said he couldn't trust me to do anything.'

There was a long pause and I remained silent until he was ready to continue.

'I was just loading up when I heard an almighty bang, followed by several others. Mackey got caught in the lot. It was all my fault.'

I tried to conceal the shock from my face, 'Mate, I'm so sorry.'

'It was put down to a tragic accident. I wasn't held accountable. I'm sure I set everything up correctly. It was down to a dud charge that was most likely tripped when he went back in. But it was still me that set it all up.' He looked over for a split second, 'It should have been me, Ben. It was my responsibility, I should have gone back in there, not him.'

'Christ, Danny. That's messed up.'

'I'm still having nightmares. Of me going back to clear up his remains. Sometimes his head is in my hands, as if he was still alive, staring up at me, eyes accusing. Other times we're sharing a cigarette, chatting as if everything is okay and then I turn and see him smeared all over the rock where he was sitting, various parts of his body at my feet. I can't take it anymore, Ben.

'I was discharged from the forces because of my leg. I messed up big time. Three of us were on a patrol just outside Kajaki about a year later. We were slowly driving through this small village in a Land Rover when I spotted a dicker in a dash-dash ride ahead of us on a moped. We all knew something wasn't right, but before we could decide what to do next, we were fired upon from all sides. For a second I just froze. It's like I switched off completely. All I could picture was Mackey's face. That's when an AK bullet shattered my kneecap, hence the permanent limp. Luckily, we managed to get out of there, but that was it for me. It was all over.

'I saw some nasty stuff while I was serving. But somehow, it just became part of the job. You kind of accepted what you did and saw it as everyday life. Kids were the worst. Seeing women and children dead or being killed tipped us all off balance a bit, but we just got on with it. That was the nature of the beast. But with Mackey, however much I tried to block him out, he kept coming back to haunt me.'

Months passed before I started to see any signs of the Danny I once knew. He never fully recovered. There was stuff going on in his head that was way beyond anything I could ever understand. I offered him a spare room at my house where he stayed for six months before getting a place of his own a few streets away. To take his mind away from his recent past, he came to work with me. He always had a talent for socialising with people which he somehow managed to keep, and putting on a brave front, he became a real asset dealing with client management. He even set up a few small businesses in Thailand after reconnecting with his mother.

He'd secured a meeting with a record company in Hamburg, and this seemed like a good time for me to return to work. We would be away for a few days, but only midweek while Kirsten was working so I didn't see any issue. She said she was okay with it, so Danny and I set about preparing our pitch. I felt an excitement I had long since forgotten existed and I believed that this would be the turning point.

The whole time we were away I was unable to reach Kirsten. I rang, left messages, and sent texts, but received no reply. With Danny's help I managed to stay focused on what we were there to do, but deep down I was beside myself with worry. On our last evening, I tried again once we got back to the hotel and this time she picked up. It was noisy on the other end of the phone as she answered with what sounded like loud voices and music. She said she was out with friends and would call me back later. I was relieved to hear her voice and tried to ignore how wasted she sounded. The trip had been successful and we'd be going home the next day, so if I could just hold on to those thoughts, I'd be fine.

As I approached the house, I saw the front door was open. I walked cautiously over the threshold, convinced I'd been burgled. The house had been trashed. Furniture was upended, picture frames smashed, vomit in the toilet and the kitchen sink. Music was trailing from somewhere down the hall and our main bedroom door was slightly ajar. The distant sound of seagulls was the first thing I heard from the open window, the curtains blowing shadows across two figures sprawled across the bed. The snoring of the guy dressed only in his boxer shorts all but dwarfed the noise of the sea. Kirsten was facing away from him, dressed only in a lace bra and knickers. There were two empty Jack Daniels bottles on the floor, joint butts in an ashtray and a large, opened bag of white powder spilling its contents over a mirrored tile.

Anger screamed at me to charge in there and unleash hell on them both, but I simply turned, stepped over the trash in the hall and went out to my car that was still parked in the garage. The door was blocked by a silver Audi TT, but the side door was clear and inside was Kirsten's red Mini and my BMW. As I approached my car, I noticed splashes of white paint on the side panel. I stared on in disbelief, and then saw that the upholstery of the front seat was slashed. I walked round to the back and was greeted by two smashed taillights and the word DICKHEAD scrawled across the number plate in thick black marker pen.

I flew back into the house screaming her name as I reached the bedroom. She sprang out of bed, not knowing where she was as the sculpted Adonis next to her stirred to life with a groan.

'Oh, you've decided to come back then?' she scoffed. No apology for the typhoon of chaos around the house or so much as an admission of guilt for her night with Mr Universe, who when he leant forward and rubbed his head with a frown, I recognised as a regular from the gym at the leisure centre.

'For Christ's sake, Kirsten. Have you seen the state of the place? What the hell is he doing here? And what's the deal with my car?'

She stared at me blankly, pushed past me and went to the bathroom, leaving me with chisel head and his hangover. He went to say something, but I saved him the bother, 'Go,' I said. He collected his clothes, stumbling to squeeze into them as he made his way to the front door.

Kirsten drifted into the kitchen wearing one of

my t-shirts, put the kettle on and began making coffee. I tried again to get some answers, 'What on earth's been going on here?'

'Let's just say I had some clients to entertain too.'

'I can't really picture Schwarzenegger doing aerobics.'

'His name is Henry, and I'm looking into starting up a personal training business.'

'Great! Why didn't you talk to me about it? And what about my car?'

'You weren't here when I needed you, Ben.'

She put a cup of coffee before me and sat opposite at the breakfast bar as I tried to right myself from the spinning, nausea-inducing motion of the Waltzer in my head.

'Kirsten, I've been nothing but good to you. I rarely go away, and on this occasion, it was to secure our future together. I love you; can't you see that?' Those three words rolled over my tongue like hot lava as I thought of Henry. I wanted to know whether she'd slept with him, and then again, I really didn't.

'Secure our future? Secure your ego you mean. You always put your business first with little consideration for me. If only you could see how your behaviour makes me feel, Ben.'

However hard she was trying to bait me into an argument, I wasn't going to get hooked any further. I could never love anyone more than her. Whatever this relationship threw at us, I was always sure we could ride out the storm. But sometimes it felt so unrequited, the life between us so laboured, that it was such a struggle to get to the next day. As she ran her fingers through her hair and turned to the light of the window, I softened, almost blurring out any of the malice she held towards me.

'I lost my job at the leisure centre. I was caught doing lines of coke by Steve.'

'Oh right, that explains a few things. Look, we always manage, don't we?' I feigned a smile, hoping it would disguise my disappointment, 'Let's get this place cleaned up. I'm sure I can get my car sorted, though I'm not looking forward to driving around with 'Dickhead' on the back.'

She nearly smiled, but then gazed into the quartz work surface where she placed her cup down. 'I'm pregnant.'

I was at a loss for words. Under such a volatile sky, what did this mean for our future? So far, the relationship had been a tangled mess and now it was at its pinnacle. In the silence that hung between us, a host of thoughts flurried for my attention, not least the concern for how Kirsten would cope with the demands of a baby.

'How do you feel?' I asked.

'I don't want it,' she replied. Despite being so resolute with her response she didn't look me in the eye.

I was going to follow up with the question, 'Is it mine?' but thought better of it. The last thing I wanted was more confrontation. Instead, I settled on, 'How far along are you?'

'Two months.'

'You know this might not be a bad thing? It could be something to focus on, to right any wrongs in the past. You could put all the good into raising this child that you missed out on when you were young.'

'I've no doubt you'd be a great father, but I'm on the verge of starting a new career in personal training. This is the last thing I wanted.'

'There's always a way, Kirsten. I'm not saying it's going to be easy, but people have kids all the time and they manage.'

'Do they Ben, or do they put all their dreams on hold indefinitely?'

I placed my hand on hers, but she pulled away, 'Think about it.'

I was helpless to know what to do.

Over a barbecue on a warm Saturday evening, I sat on the beach with Danny, looking to him for advice. 'Mate, you've got to be crazy. She's just going to ruin the kid's life on top of yours. I'm going to be the best friend I can possibly be by telling you to get shot of her. She's a psycho!'

I threw a flat stone into the incoming tide, 'Don't mince your words will you.'

'Somebody's got to tell you. You're the only one who can't see what she's doing to you. She's messing with your head. This is not you. Not the guy I've known since school.' He took a swig from his bottle of Becks. 'I used to look up to you and I've always seen you as the brother I never had. You're the smartest one out of us two and the most positive. Well, you used to be. You're nothing but a disaster now.'

'Thanks for that.'

'You'd be so much better without her.'

I was about to respond when we heard crunching of pebbles behind us. We simultaneously turned to see Kirsten standing above us, hands on hips, 'Really? Is that what you think, Ben?'

She stormed into the house, retrieved a bottle of Smirnoff from her bag and a carton of orange juice from the fridge and began to pour.

'Nice little team you two make. You've both got it in for me, haven't you?'

'Of course not,' I said. 'He's just had a little too much to drink.'

I tried to put my hand out to comfort her and distract her from the glass, but she moved into the living room and downed the drink in one.

'Get him out of here. Now!'

I slid open the patio doors but didn't have to say anything. Danny was already making his way towards the side of the house, 'I'll catch up with you later, Ben,' he said, and got into his car.

'He's got a bloody nerve. All we've done for him, and he treats us like this.'

'He's gone now. Try and calm down, for the baby's sake.'

I slid the bottle away, but she grabbed it before I got the chance and swung it, hitting me hard on my right cheek.

Bottle in hand she stared down at me as I cradled my face.

'I don't want him in this house again, do you hear?'

Side stepping me, she marched off towards the bedroom.

I knew there would be no resolve until she calmed down. Anything I did now would only make the situation worse. Instead, I hovered by the door and called out meekly, 'I'm going out for a bit, I'll be back soon.'

'That's it, you go and join him. I don't know why you don't ask him to move in and get rid of me. You're obviously made for each other.'

She said something else, but I didn't hear. I was already out of the door and on my way to A&E. A lengthy wait in the emergency room should supply the space we both needed.

I returned home to find her gone. When I looked in the bedroom, I saw a pile of my clothes strewn across the bed and the floor, and most of her things missing. I tried to call her mobile, but it kept going to voicemail. I texted her to ask if she was okay. It was hours before she finally replied with, 'Now you can be happy. I won't be back.'

Three days later after not hearing a thing, I went to see her friend Jade to see if she was staying there. Jade's eyes widened as she opened the door, 'Christ Ben, what happened to you?'

My face was a dark purple down on one side and

swollen like a balloon.

'Took a fall running along the beach a couple of days ago.' The same excuse I gave to the hospital. 'Is Kirsten here?'

'She's been staying with Tel. It may not be my place, and Kirsten will kill me if she finds out, but she, er...'

'Jade, just tell me.'

'She's planning on having an abortion.'

'What? Where?'

'Marie Stopes, in London I think.'

I thanked her, left her to close the door and got straight on the phone to Louise.

'Oh Ben, I'm so sorry. Do you think it might be best to leave her to it?'

'No, I don't. You know I want this child. If only we could try.'

'I know, but it's her decision at the end of the day.'

'Why is it? I know she must carry the baby and give birth, but surely, I have a say in this too?'

'Is she still staying with Jade's ex?'

'Tel? You knew?'

'Danny knows Jade from the gym. I didn't want to say anything, I was hoping she'd calm down. She always comes back to you. I didn't realise it had gone this far though.'

'Where does he live? Is she seeing him?'

'I can't say for sure. I know they've got quite close, and let's face it, he earns quite a bit.'

'Now's not the time, Louise. Where does he live?'

'I'm not sure it's wise you going round there in this state. I'm off to a function with Greg tonight, but I'll pop over there first thing in the morning.'

'That'll be great. Are you sure you don't mind?'

'Leave it with me. I'll call you tomorrow.'

I knew Kirsten didn't have much time for my sister, but Louise had a calming way with people. If anyone could talk Kirsten out of this, I hoped it would be her.

I received a call shortly after nine the following morning. Louise broke the news that Kirsten was on her way to the clinic. Before I had a chance to say anything in response, she informed me that she was in the car with Danny on the way to Brixton to talk with her.

'Is it sensible going with Danny?'

'It was the only way I could get there. Greg's using my car as his is in for a service today. It was either that or I ask you to take me, and I don't think that's a wise idea the state you're in. Don't worry, she won't know he's around, I've told him to make himself scarce.'

I sat in wait as the hours passed painstakingly slow. Finally, after midday I received a call from Danny, 'Mate, I'm so sorry about the other day. That was insensitive of me.'

'Forgotten. Any news?'

'Yeah. Louise has just texted me to say she's on her way back to the car. Kirsten's not going through with it.'

If I needed confirmation of how I felt about

Kirsten and the baby, it was there and then. There was no doubt in my mind I needed them both in my life.

God knows how she made it to nine months. On the day of the birth when she was rushed into hospital, I could only pray that both her and our little girl would be safe. My concern was given full justification when Emma was born with asphyxia. I hung from tenterhooks as the nurses rallied around to resuscitate her. But from the very beginning Emma was a fighter. A little cough and the most wonderful noise I'd ever heard of her crying signified my life was about to change for forever.

But from the moment we left the hospital, Kirsten wanted nothing to do with Emma. I hoped that she would eventually bond with her, but she spent so little time at home, I couldn't see how that was ever going to happen. I assumed the responsibility for taking care of her and was more than happy to do so. Emma was incredible.

Nothing could have prepared me for just how challenging taking care of a baby could be. I was lucky. Emma was a great sleeper, and although she cried at various times throughout the night, she'd settle down soon enough once I figured out what she needed. Whether it was winding or feeding her or just have her watch me with great amusement as she projectile vomited over me while I changed her nappy – we made a great little team. My sleep was disrupted, and I was the most exhausted and emotional I'd ever been in my entire life, but I wouldn't have changed a thing.

Surprisingly, I enjoyed work more, spurred on by the sense of purpose and responsibility Emma brought to my life. I could conduct most things like meetings, client conversations and dealings at the office with the use of video conferencing, and Danny managed everything else including supervising the creative team. He was by my side constantly to help with Emma when he wasn't working, and with the addition of Louise, Greg, and my parents to chip in support, Emma and I were made.

I begged for Kirsten to be a part of Emma's life, but the sheer thought of motherhood abandoned her. I found it unbelievable she would shun her own daughter like this, she didn't even want to hold her. I wondered if it was postnatal depression, but other than her reluctance to bond with Emma, she didn't display any other symptoms. Kirsten was busy with her personal fitness and quite driven with her business plans. She was happy leaving me to it and as a couple we were living very separate lives. Coming and going as she pleased, often staying away for days at a time, Kirsten was more like a part time lodger than a member of our nuclear family.

For me, as I got to know my beautiful girl, I knew my love was enough to carry her all the way through life for as long as I lived. I adored her, spending my days playing with her, tending to her every need, wiping the tears from my eyes when she said her very first word, 'Dada', and watching her stumble as she took her first steps. We'd come such a long way together. I could hardly remember my life without her.

By the time Emma had reached four years old, I was fully in the swing of parenthood. Every now and then Kirsten helped with a few things such as shopping and a little washing, but where hands on parenting was concerned, her absence was normal.

She came home late one evening, at around 11.30. I'd dozed off with Emma in my arms. She'd had a nightmare where she was chased by a tree. I made her some warm milk and settled her down with a book that I read to her until her eyes gently closed. Kirsten went to say something, but I interrupted with a whisper, 'Let me just put Emma to bed and I'll be right with you.'

Emma stirred a little, but soon found comfort under her duvet and slipped back into her dreams with ease. I walked into the kitchen where Kirsten was pouring a shot of vodka.

'I've been offered a full-time place in Henry's Gym,' she announced. I thought she would be overjoyed by the news, but there was an undertone that told me that there was more on its way, 'It's in Tampa, Florida.'

'I knew he was American, but I didn't know he owned a business out there. You said no, right?' As soon as I said it out loud, I already knew the answer.

'I said yes,' she replied above a whisper.

'But what about me and Emma?'

'You've been doing a brilliant job of raising her, and let's face it, you and I haven't been getting on for a while.'

I couldn't believe what I was hearing. It was almost as if I was in a bubble and couldn't decipher her words.

'Kirsten, you can't go. You can't leave us. She's your daughter. Why can't you get a job here? Please...'

I suddenly heard my own voice in my head, how pathetic I must have sounded pleading like a child.

'Ben don't make this harder than it already is. My decision is made. I fly in two weeks.'

'But...'

'You and Emma will be fine. I'm staying with Tel until I go. He's outside now. I'm going to pack a few things and I'll be back tomorrow to get the rest while you're out.'

Whether it was lack of sleep or the whole emotional roller-coaster I'd been on with Kirsten, I couldn't say, but as soon as she started packing an overnight bag, I lost all control and tears fell like rain. 'Please, think about this. Everything you could ever need is here, with us.'

'I'm sorry, Ben. I'm sorry for hurting you and I'm sorry it didn't all work out into the fairy-tale you spun in your head. I'm just not cut out for this. Tell Emma I love her.'

My sorrow switched to anger in a second, 'You love her? If you loved her, you would have held her when she was crying, you would have looked after her when she needed you the most. If you loved her, you wouldn't be leaving her.'

'Let's not do this now, Ben. You're clearly upset and unable to see sense.'

'See sense? I see this clearly for what it is. You're selfish and only care about yourself. Me, me, me, that's all you see.'

'I think you've said enough.'

She left the bedroom, a holdall filled with her things. I reached out and grabbed her arm, 'Kirsten, I'm sorry.'

'Let go.' I dropped my hand as she opened the door, 'Goodbye Ben.'

I stood by, helpless, as I watched her get into Tel's car. He didn't look over. Instead, he placed the bag on the back seat and started the car as if I wasn't there.

I closed the front door to a silence so still it made me physically ache.

9

The roar of the plane muffles the best part of surrounding conversation. To my relief the seat alongside me is empty. Breakfast is served in a colourful plastic tie-bag: a black bread sandwich, a carton of orange juice and a square of tangy lemon cake. I've taken the risk of bringing the rest of the hashish with me, along with a full bottle of vodka. My head is clear, but is crying out to be subdued, for the babble to cease, and the angst to ease. I become nauseous as I finish the food and dry retch at the window. My nerves push me closer to the edge as the man behind me continuously kicks my seat.

When I'm finally out on the street, I grab the nearest people carrier into a quiet part of town on the recommendation of the driver. The hotel is basic to say the least, but I need for no more. My mood is softened by the sight of two resident cats dressed in little hoodies, before the irritating manager returns me to concrete. He splutters over my passport, his lungs congested from years of smoking. I swipe it back, wipe it on my trouser leg and throw him a frown. He tries to go with me to my room, but I leave before he has the chance.

I dump my backpack on the floor and delve straight into my shoulder bag, roll a joint, pour a generous glass of vodka, head to the balcony and let out a sigh. In the shadow of lush green hills, the air is cooler, clearer and I welcome the slight breeze. I feel the urban claustrophobia of Bangkok leaving my body. Basking in the sunshine for a few hours, I give in to the peace. Before the full onset of intoxication has taken hold, I reach for my phone.

'Hello?'

'Hello darling, how are you?'

'Daddy! Aunty Louise, it's daddy.'

'What are you doing answering the phone?'

'Aunty Louise said I could. I knew it would be you.'

'What are you up to?'

'We're making chocolate muffins to take to the beach.'

'Are you now? You know if you eat too many, you'll lose your two front teeth?'

'You're so silly, daddy. The tooth fairy took those two weeks ago, remember?'

'Oh yes, that's right. And do you still have the money you saved to spend today?'

'Yeah, I put it in my piggy bank. Aunty Louise and

me are going to the book shop later, so I'll probably spend it there.'

'That's good, sweetheart. Listen, I can't stay for long and I'm sure your aunty will need you in the kitchen soon.'

'When will I see you again?'

'Soon, beautiful, soon.'

'Okay. I miss you lots and lots.'

'Me too. I love you.'

'Love you, daddy.'

I stare at the blank screen for what feels like a lifetime and then place the mobile on the table next to me. She's my only way out. The escape from the corners in the shadows of my mind. Before she came into my life, I was simply ambling along with no clear direction. She gave me purpose, a point to everything, a million reasons to strive and believe there was more to life that what I could physically see. I fill another glass, light another joint, reach out for a lifeline from the swell within.

When I wake, I run straight to the bathroom and throw up, the vodka acid scarring my throat upon its return. Inside my head, an ache thumps maniacally, like my brain is trying to break free from my skull. I hear ringing and glance over to my phone, the screen dancing to the noise.

'Danny,' I answer.

'How're you doing? You all settled in? Found a hotel?'

'Yeah. What's new?'

'I'm having trouble tying down my contact, he keeps giving me the run around. Don't worry, he's sound, just a bit unreliable with timekeeping.'

I pause before I answer, 'Am I wasting my time? I'm not here for a holiday you know. The longer I leave this, the harder it gets.'

'I know, and I appreciate that, but I promise I'm doing my best. Have you found out where she is yet?'

'No. Her fiancée has rented a villa in the hills somewhere. I saw a post on Facebook and Instagram, but apart from that, no leads.'

'Just keep your head down and I'll see what I can do. In the meantime, carry on snooping online and try to gain as much info as possible. Every little helps. You need to keep a close eye on her without being seen yourself. If it all comes through this end, then you'll have to move straight away.'

'I hope it's sooner rather than later. I'm not sure how much more of this I can take.'

'Sure. I'll be in touch.'

The thought of venturing out fills me with a dread so thick I can barely breathe. Lying in bed is my only desire. I gulp down a large mouthful of vodka, followed by another. The engulfing fire in my throat and chest is instant. I open my mouth to take in gulps of cool air and catch only swirling figments of what should have been and all that's lost. I distract myself by making a spliff, allowing the rising monster of my tangled morass to drift back to sleep.

A strip of hazy sunlight pierces the gap in the curtain. I rub my eyes and feel a dull ache for the day ahead. Taxis here don't seem to run as they do in Bangkok. The alternative are red pick-ups that are shared with others, squeezed in like canned goods in a supermarket aisle. It's far from appealing. I call Danny and ask if he knows of any trustworthy car rental firms. The conversation is stunted, as if I shouldn't be bothering him. He tells me he'll send someone to pick me up from my hotel.

I have no idea how to track her down and with no information from Danny, I'm left with very little to do. The fifty something driver arrives – slim built, impeccably dressed, apart from a pair of questionable worn-out tan sandals. His name is Kasem. Originally from Bangkok, he now works as a private driver in Chiang Mai. I ask him to take me away into the hills. I'm hoping the fresh air will alleviate some of the compression of the room.

About an hour into the drive, he pulls over, 'Please, come. I have something to show.'

I feel like I'm being led into another robbery scenario, but I could never have guessed what he had in mind. After walking for ten minutes or so through a dense forest, we arrive in a clearing of thatched bamboo huts. Children play and women work at hand looms. The ladies have tight brass coils wrapped around their necks; a smaller number of coils for the girls elevating in length as age progresses until the elderly are seen with abnormally elongated necks. I can't help but stare in fascination, wondering how on earth it's at all possible.

'This Kayen long neck tribe from Myanmar. Here they make shawl and other gift for tourist people.' Kasem pauses to drag on his cigarette, 'If you wan, I ask if you wanna buy something.'

I decline. I only came for the drive and not to stare at these people as I find myself doing. I smile at a lady and her child amid a wash of multi-coloured fabric and head back to the car.

'Can we get a good view of the hills somewhere?' I ask instead. We wind around the bends for twenty minutes until he stops the car at a ridge overlooking the highlands dipping into a lush basin of forestry. A line of young men dressed in dirty brown vests and knee length shorts stride past, balancing twined branches upon their heads. Kasem tries his best to fish information from me – simple questions of my country of origin, what I do for a living and so on, but he soon tires of the short replies. We sit instead in silence with only far away bird song and the limitless vista.

By late afternoon I return to the hotel for a quick shower before I'm out again for something to eat. I head into the city centre, quite the contrast from the silence of the road where my hotel is situated. Designer shops and western fast-food restaurants line the streets. Wandering hawkers try relentlessly to sell their wares to whoever is willing enough to fall for their charms. I find a Thai restaurant filled half with tourists, half with locals and eat a questionable green curry. Night has fallen by the time I leave, and I head for a bar, noisy and intrusive. Outside a couple of Germans are flirting with two tall Thai women in short skirts. At least they're convinced they are women. I think they may be in for an unwanted surprise later.

With several beers sunk, I step out of the bar, looking at my phone as I walk. My peripheral catches a figure, but it's too late and I collide into a man reeking of expensive cologne. My phone clatters to the floor and I curse under my breath. The person apologises in a heavy European accent. I pick up my handset. It's still working, no real damage, just a slight dent in the corner. My patience is about to burst when I realise it's Rodrigo. I keep my head down, mumble an apology myself and move on. He doesn't seem to know who I am or recognise me, but then why would he? I turn a corner and watch from a distance as Kirsten leaves a clothes store, several bags in hand to join him. I follow at a distance, keeping myself hidden amongst the crowds. They stop to embrace. I turn, pretending to admire a small dog sat in a basket attached to a bicycle.

I tail them until they're at a main road. It's then I see Kasem leaning against his car. I'd completely forgotten I'd asked him to pick me up. I get in the back and ask him to follow the Range Rover they've driven away in. It's over half an hour before it stops at the rented villa I'd seen on Facebook, even more luxurious than the pictures depict. We've parked far enough away not to be seen. I don't get out, but instead stare on, wondering what life must be like for her now. Kasem tells me he's memorised the address and can bring me back anytime. I'm starting to like him.

The following evening the villa is in darkness. I walk around the high walls looking for a way in. Around the back, under the shadow of a hillock is a side entrance and I'm surprised to find the gate unlatches with ease. The gentle lapping water in the swimming pool is the only sound. Kasem has no idea what I'm up to. I asked him to text me if there are any signs of cars approaching.

The windows are bare, the rooms within lit by moonlight. A silver sheen on the floors makes it easy to distinguish the shadows of each interior. It's a one storey building, glass on all sides. A huge living area with equally large kitchen and five bedrooms with what seems to be ensuite bathrooms leading from all. The space is immaculate. There's no doubt they have hired staff: cleaners, maybe a cook and a gardener too. The property certainly wouldn't be looked after by her.

A whirring catches my attention as I turn the corner to the front of the villa. I look up to see a panning surveillance camera and retreat just in time before it lands on me. Circling the house back in the opposite direction, I see if I can find any more, but it appears to be the only one. I look through the kitchen window at the rippled marble worktops, shiny chrome fittings, six cooking hobs and an oversized refrigerator. It's then I spot the lazy flashing light on a plastic box attached to the wall. Another grabs my attention in the hallway leading to the front door. I can only assume an alarm system of sorts. I feel as if at any moment I might step on a floor panel and set off a siren. My heart leaps to the sound of a vibrating text alert. I slink back into the hedgerows, kneel, and check my phone under the cover of my cupped hand. 'CAR COME.'

Keeping rigid against the back wall with the hedges as the only cover, I can see clearly to the front gates. They open slowly to an automatic floodlight that reveals the entire property. A black Mercedes drives slowly past me towards twin garages I hadn't noticed before. One of the doors opens and the car is swallowed.

A few minutes later the house is illuminated. I'm sure I can't be seen, but I don't risk it by moving. Rodrigo is the first person to appear. He casually moves through the kitchen to the living area, places a set of keys on a luxurious coffee table in the middle of four tanned leather sofas and continues to open the double doors to the swimming pool and garden. He stands and breathes in the night air. He's dressed smartly: jeans, slightly unbuttoned white shirt; the light catching his loafers.

Stress rises in my chest as I see Kirsten come up behind him, wrapping her arms around his waist. He responds by turning and pulling her into a firm embrace. He whispers in her ear, and she laughs.

Walking over to a drawer, he pulls out a handheld remote control and what I thought was merely mahogany panelling, opens to reveal an entertainment unit to the likes I could never imagine. A television the size of a cinema screen takes centre stage, below separate units light up like the control panel of a spaceship. He places the remote back in the drawer, voice commands music and the sound of Claude Debussy's *Clair de Lune* fills the air.

I stifle a laugh as she tries to dance like a ballerina around the sofas.

'You are sheer grace, my love,' he remarks as his eyes follow her.

I know I must leave, but I find myself magnetised. She falls into his arms with perfect timing, leaning back as he bends to kiss her.

'Thank you for a wonderful evening,' she says, never taking her eyes from his. 'Maybe we can return tomorrow.'

'You would not like to eat somewhere else?' he replies, pulling her up, his hands in hers.

'I really liked it there. The staff were so nice. It's as if they've known us for years. And like you said, they're the only place that serves such great Italian in Chiang Mai.'

She pulls him close, leans her head to the side of his chest and stares out. I fall back against the wall. For a split second it's as if she's staring directly at me, then she separates and enters the master bedroom while he slides into the kitchen and pours red wine into two oversized glasses. She reappears in a black cherry negligee, leaving little to the imagination. He glides like a puppet into the bedroom, kicking the door shut behind him.

I've seen enough. The nausea inside concocts with fury, the pressure of seeing her with him in their enchanted bubble so soon fit to burst. The nerves of creeping around like a burglar have now gone. I saunter out the way I came in as if it were my own home, leaving the gate wide open without a care.

Kasem bites his nails and spits what's discarded to the breeze. He opens the door as I approach and we make haste, driving back to the hotel where the warm embrace of insobriety is waiting to hold me so dear.

10

The rusted leaves scattered upon the open lawns of Sandgate Park showed the first signs of autumn, that and the skeleton of locals exposed from the heave of summer tourists newly departed for another year. A huddle of smokers gathered at the corner of The Ship Inn. The spirals of smoke mixed with the waft of freshly cooked fish and chips from the takeaway opposite. A few passers-by glanced through the dusty windows of the antique shops. Other than them there is only traffic, the squawks of hungry seagulls and the wash of threatening waves to break the silence.

Emma and I had been on our own for just over a year. Every day we'd walk hand in hand along the sea front and end up at Manuel's for a juice and a coffee, sometimes a slice of cake. The restaurant where Kirsten and I had had our first date was a cafe in the daytime and became a regular place Emma and I would hang out.

The staff at Manuel's had become quite fond of us. The owner, Manuel, who had a strong Spanish accent, always had Emma in a fit of giggles by pulling funny faces or doing silly things to entertain her. Along with his son and the two waitresses, they made our visits feel like a home away from home. It was also somewhere to distract me from what Kirsten was doing on the other side of the Atlantic. In the whole time she'd been away, she hadn't called once. It was clear she had washed her hands of us both, and although I was coming to terms with it, each day felt like an uphill struggle. Despite everything, I still loved and missed her so much.

I'd managed to juggle things so I could run the company effectively with the help of Danny. Emma was doing well in day care, so that gave me some extra time to focus on the business. Sometimes, when I'd wait outside Tiny Tots Day Care for Emma to finish, I'd talk with one of the mothers, Naomi. So far it had been nothing more than idle chit-chat.

It was a Tuesday afternoon, and it hadn't long stopped raining. We were both soaked through. The little ones were painting autumn pictures today and from what I could tell, there would be three prizes for the best ones.

'So, have you had all the buzz around the painting?' I asked Naomi.

She pulled a brush from her handbag and tried to detangle her wet auburn hair.

WHAT WE BECOME

'It's all I've heard about all week,' she laughed.

'I'm not sure who's more excited, me or Emma.'

'Yeah, it means so much to them at that age. I think it's good though, for them to try hard at something like this. Isabelle really loves her art.'

'Emma too. She's always grabbing her paint brushes or my camera, and anything she can lay her hands on to make something out of. Whether it's egg cartons, pieces of card, you name it.'

'You can't keep your eyes off them for a second, huh?'

'You're not wrong there. Hey, do you fancy grabbing a coffee?'

No sooner had I said it, had guilt started gnawing at my conscience. It was like I was going behind Kirsten's back.

'Um, Uh...' She was at a loss for words, and who could blame her.

'I'm sorry, that was a bit forward of me.'

My face flushed with embarrassment.

'No, not at all. You just caught me by surprise that's all.' She looked down at Isabelle who was standing patiently, twirling one of her chestnut pigtails. 'Do you fancy some coffee, Izzy?'

'Can we have biscuits?'

'Hmmm, only a few. We wouldn't want to spoil dinner now, would we now?'

'Okay,' Isabelle beamed.

Emma came running out with a rolled piece of paper in her hand, 'Daddy, look.'

'Oh, that's beautiful darling,' I replied, unfurling

a scene of red and brown leaf mayhem before my eyes. 'But who did this masterpiece?'

'Me and Isabelle,' Emma replied looking puzzled.

'Really?'

'Yes.'

'I thought you stole it from a famous art gallery.'

'No, I promise. We did it.'

'How amazing. It looks like a professional artist painted it.' I winked at Naomi. 'And did you win a prize?'

'Yeah.'

Both Isabelle and Emma jumped up and down.

'We won two cinema tickets,' squealed Isabelle.

'Wow, well done girls, good on you. Now settle down and put your coats on,' Naomi said. The girls ran ahead. 'I'm sure we'll hear all about it over coffee. You're so good with Emma by the way. She's lucky to have such a great dad.'

'Oh thanks.' I blushed with pride, looking at my wonderful daughter as she skipped ahead.

We strolled into Manuel's to a cheeky grin from Helen, one of the waitresses. Whilst Naomi and Isabelle settled down at a table, I went to the counter to order.

'New friends?' Helen asked.

'Naomi and Isabelle? Yeah, we met at day care.'

'They're lovely. They come in here quite a bit. She's single you know.'

'Really? I mean, why would I want to know that?'

'Your secret is safe with me, Ben,' she chuckled.

I returned with our drinks and a plate of

chocolate chip cookies.

'Emma's the same age as Izzy, isn't she?' Naomi asked as I sat down.

'Five going on eighteen,' I laughed. 'I'm surprised how quick she's grown.'

I reached into my wallet and retrieved a worn picture of her from when she was two.

'Oh, she's beautiful. One minute they're in nappies, the next minute they're bossing you around the house.'

'Tell me about it. But she's everything I am. I can't imagine life without her.'

'How sweet. Her mum must be very proud of her.'

'We're not together. She lives in America.'

'That must be hard, parenting on your own.'

'It can be at times, but I get plenty of support from friends and family. How about you?'

'My mum and sister help out and I've got a few friends who share babysitting nights so we can have a little time to ourselves. To be honest though, the second Izzy's away, I miss her like crazy.'

'Same here. Sometimes when they're running around your feet, you'd kill for a break and as soon as they're away, you can't wait for them to come home again.'

I lingered for a second longer than maybe I should have, looking into the sapphire of her eyes. I wasn't sure what I felt in that moment, but it was like a wound-up spring inside of me suddenly let loose and was bouncing around my chest. I looked away and to the steamed windows.

'So, what is it you do for a living, Ben? Or do you spend all your time looking after Emma?'

'I have my own business. A creative agency.'

'How do you manage to run a business and look after Emma? I struggle with just Isabelle.'

'We get by. I've got some people working for me and once she starts school full-time, I'll have extra time to be more hands on.'

'Where's Emma going?'

'Seabrook Primary.'

'Oh, Izzy's going there too. It's such a wonderful school.'

'I've heard nothing but great things. It's small, but the teachers are fantastic. I know the head quite well, Mr Canning. I wish I had had a head of school like that when I was her age.'

'Yeah, he's great. He's always smiling and very caring, and the kids think the world of him.'

'I guess we'll be seeing more of each other then.'

'I hope so. Maybe we could meet up for a play date or something. Isabelle loves Emma.'

'That'd be great.'

'Daddy, look at our picture,' Emma interrupted, holding the painting out.

'That's awesome. Is that a tree?'

The girls nodded simultaneously and smiled.

'We won a cinema ticket,' Emma said.

'Really? You didn't tell me that,' I laughed. 'What are you going to see?'

'I don't know yet.' She slurped some apple juice

and continued talking to Isabelle.

'Are you busy on Sunday?' Naomi asked.

'This Sunday. I don't think so, why?'

'I was going to take Izzy to Howletts. Do you fancy joining us.'

'What do you say Emma, do you want to see the animals?'

'Yes please, daddy. Can we see the elephants and rhinos?'

'I'm sure we can.'

When Sunday arrived, I was in a fluster. Emma was taking forever to choose her outfit and I was surprisingly nervous. I shouldn't have been. Naomi and I got along very well, and I felt at ease in her company, but if I was honest, I was really attracted to her. When I told Danny and Louise about her, they were thrilled. They said that it was about time I found someone who was good for us. But I still felt as if I was betraying Kirsten, despite reassurances to the contrary.

Naomi looked amazing. She had a little make up on, which I hadn't seen her wear before. Not that she needed it, she was naturally beautiful. She wore stylish jeans and a baggy red and brown jumper with a matching scarf, whilst Isabelle was dressed in an assortment of blues including a little bobble hat.

'I'm wearing my zookeepers' clothes,' Emma informed Naomi, standing with her chest puffed out and displaying her Lion King sweatshirt I bought from the Disney Store. 'RAOORR!'

'Roar to you too, young lady,' laughed Naomi. 'You look like you'll keep all those wild animals in line.'

'Look Mr Langley, I'm wearing my rain clothes to keep the rain away,' Isabelle said, and puffed her chest out so her jacket burst open to reveal a little blonde cartoon girl with an umbrella under a rainbow.

'So you are. And does this little girl have a name?' I said pointing to her jumper.

'Yes. This is Jessica the Rainbow Princess.'

We shuffled in line to the ticket kiosk and had to tear the girls away from the gift shop.

'We'll have a look on the way back,' Naomi said. 'If we don't go now, all the animals will fall asleep.'

The girls looked at each other and Emma said, 'We better go Isabelle, come on.'

Isabelle grabbed Emma's hand and they ran ahead of us through the doors to the park.

'Stay close now. Make sure you can always see us,' I instructed, but it fell on deaf ears.

We ambled along while girls were transfixed by the black and white colobus monkeys. Emma had my old phone which she used for taking pictures. Naomi and I laughed so much when they posed for a selfie with the monkeys in the background.

I pointed over to the opposite enclosure, 'Shall we take a look at the lions and tigers?'

'Yes please. Where are they?' Emma asked.

'Right behind you. Look.'

Through the mesh and behind a tree was a

Barbary lion basking in the sunshine.

I read from the information board attached to the fencing, 'The Barbary lion has been extinct in the wild since the 1940s with only around one hundred of this subspecies still existing in captivity around the world.'

'What does extinct mean?' Isabelle asked.

'The species has no more living members in the wild. It may have died due to loss of habitat or may have been hunted until there were no more left,' Naomi replied.

'Like some of the rhinos?' Emma added.

'That's right.'

'Let's see the silly anteaters,' Emma said, taking hold of Isabelle's hand.

'They're good together, aren't they?' Naomi commented.

'Absolutely, a great little team.'

With Emma's rucksack over my shoulder, my hands were in my pockets to keep them warm. Naomi put her hand through the loop of my arm, 'It's a bit chilly, do you mind?'

'Be my guest.'

We sat down at a picnic area and organised the contents of the rucksacks on the table for lunch while the girls played on the swings.

'So, what do you guys get up to in your spare time?' Naomi asked as she opened a packet of cheese and onion crisps.

'We visit my mum and dad's, my sister and her husband, or Danny, my friend comes over. He's known as Uncle Danny to Emma, they're thick as thieves. He loves her like his own. We do the usual things: walks along the beach, playgrounds, go shopping, that sort of thing. Every Saturday afternoon we dress up and go out to dinner and then catch a film.'

'We do the same sort of stuff, but we haven't done the dressing up for dinner thing yet, sounds ace.'

'Yeah, it is. You'll have to join us. It's a lot of fun. But it takes all morning for her to get ready,' I laughed.

'I bet. Girls, hey? Do you ever hear from Kirsten?'

The mention of her name made my stomach tilt. If only she was like Naomi, what a wonderful mother she would have made.

'No. Not a thing. She was never cut out for it all unfortunately. She didn't even care when Emma said her first words, took her first steps or rode her bike for the first time. Those firsts were everything to me. I love the way Emma is so smart and picks up on all I say and has a question for everything.'

'Oh, they're great like that, but it can get a little tiresome sometimes,' she laughed.

'Too true, they can be a handful alright, but I wouldn't change it for the world.'

I was relieved the conversation had steered back to the children. I was having such an enjoyable time and I didn't want the interruption of Kirsten to sour the day.

After we'd seen the honey badgers, clouded

leopards, Sumatran, Indian and Amur tigers, the northern Chinese leopards and snow leopards, we headed to the elephant and eastern black rhino enclosures where Emma told Isabelle more about the northern whites.

'You've not got anyone special in your life?' I asked Naomi.

'A partner? No. David left us when I was six months pregnant, and I haven't seen him since. It's just me and Izzy against the world.' She smiled warmly at me.

When it was time to leave, the girls spent ages in the gift shop, picking toys and books up, and looking over to us to ensure we'd seen their expressions of interest. Emma held a colouring book and a clip-on tiger tail, whilst Isabelle held a purple rubber snake and a clip-on lemur tail. I paid for them at the counter.

'You didn't have to do that.' Naomi said, rummaging around her bag for her purse, 'Let me give you the money back.'

I held up my hand, 'Honestly, it was my pleasure. It's been a breath of fresh air for both of us.'

'Thank you, we've had a lovely day.'

The afternoon graduated into a rich golden sunset with a clear star-filled sky close behind. We ate dinner at Naomi's and Emma stayed over. Once the girls were asleep, Naomi and I snuggled up on the sofa and ended up falling asleep to Love Actually on the television. I woke in the middle of the night, somewhere around three and turned the TV off and resumed my position in her arms. I couldn't remember being this happy.

11

I make it as far as the stairwell but turn and rush back to my room, reaching for the bottle before I close the door behind me. The bitter whisky causes me to retch, and I steady myself on the bureau to slow my heart pounding war with my chest. I grab a cigarette but decide on a joint as the alcohol paces its way through my system. After the fifth drag, my legs give way and I fall, hitting my head on the corner of the desk. Pain detonates with such an intensity I can hardly breathe as the embers of the spliff glow in and out of focus.

Separating the side of my face from the pool of blood on the floor, I wince at the stinging around my left temple. The damage reflected in the mirror isn't as bad as I feared. I scrub away caked claret from my face, and I'm left with only a small cut above my eye, a purpling bump underneath. The joint stares up at me from the end of the bed and I lift it to my mouth and light it, inhale deeply, cough uncontrollably and lean back into the duvet. With my other hand I withdraw from my wallet a small photograph of Emma. She'd just had her hair cut when this was taken. She was so happy with how it looked, the biggest smile sweeping across her face. I wasn't so sure at first, only because I loved her long blonde hair. It had been time for a change though and a shorter crop was more fashionable. She looked beautiful, her face the kind that could carry any style and this one made her bright blue eyes come alive. I'm absorbed by her staring back at me.

I remove the bandage from my arm and run the flame of the lighter up and down the old seeping wounds, screwing my eyes tight with the searing bite until I can't take any more. Just enough not to do too much damage, but enough to reap the physical when all the emotional is numb. Tomorrow I'll work on the other arm, giving the blisters a little time to heal. My clothes hide my scars well. Rolling around the dregs of Mekhong, I swig the bottle back, leaving it lying on the bed as I dress to leave. Kasem is waiting by a white Toyota when I step out.

'Ah Mr Ben, a very fine morning,' he chirps.

'Take me to a temple, please. Somewhere where there's lots of people?'

I'm caught in a conundrum. Although my paranoia will be on overload, I need the distraction, the break from myself.

'Of course. We go to Doi Suthep, very nice place.'

The winding drive takes us high into the hills where workers clean litter from the roadside and school children on excursions study the flora. When we arrive, I realise he wasn't wrong about it being one of the most popular temples in Chiang Mai. Souvenir shops seek advantage of the tourists oblivious to the traffic at the base of the three hundred or so steps leading to the summit entrance. I clamber out into the scorching heat and gradually ascend the staircase bordered each side by decorative water serpent balustrades. People selfishly budge past and halfway up I take a breath, the alcohol and smoking taking its toll. I feel pity for the locals who simply wish to worship, disrupted by these travellers, many of whom show so little respect for this sacred place, talking loudly and throwing litter everywhere. It's stifling and overbearing, and although I wanted to be amongst people, I'm not sure I want to be here. By the time I've circled the towering gold chedi, browsed the pagodas, statues of Buddha in varying poses and the colourful shrines, I feel like I'm suffocating. I try to relax by looking out from a long promenade to the spectacular views over the city spreading out for miles, but crowds pushing up against me, impatient for my position, have me rushing down the stairs and back to the car, panting and perspiring from the glaring faces.

Kasem laughs and says, 'Yes, yes, many step, very hard climb.'

I sit at the bottom of my bed on the cool tiled floor. With tremoring hands, I pour a drink while battling the voices constantly nagging me with every fine detail I try to avoid. Begging for distraction, I get changed, go out to buy two more bottles of Mekhong and go back to my room. I drown myself in alcohol until the words become a jumble and the numbness takes hold.

'Hello?'

'Louise, hi, how's things?'

'All okay here. You sound like you've had better days though. Do you want to talk to Emma?'

'That'd be good. Thanks again for taking care of her.'

'It's no problem. I love spending time with her. Hold on a minute, I'll go and get her. She's reading in her room. Emma, it's your dad on the phone.'

'Daddy! I miss you.'

'I miss you too, beautiful. So, did you have a good day at the beach? Make any sandcastles?'

'No, but I found a dead jellyfish.'

'Oh lovely! You didn't touch it though?'

'No, it was too weird and jellyfied.'

'Jellyfied? That's a new one. What else did you do?'

'We went paddling in the sea and we played tennis with the plastic bats from the garden.'

'Well, well, the next Maria Sharapova.'

'Huh?'

'Never mind. So, did you go to the bookshop?'

'No. I'm going to go tomorrow. I was having so much fun at the seaside and Aunty Louise said it was time for tea. We had ham and cheese sandwiches, and Aunty Louise made me my own strawberry jellyfish. It was so cool. It wobbled and everything.'

'That's great, darling. I wish I was there.'

'Are you coming home now?'

'Soon darling, soon. You give Aunty Louise a big kiss and cuddle before bed and say thank you.'

'I will. You're going now, aren't you?'

'Yeah, but hey, how many times have I left you before this time?'

'Never.'

'And I promise never to leave you again. I love you, sweetheart.'

'Love you too, daddy.

Kasem pulls up behind a long line of expensive cars near the villa. There's a steady thud of dance music as I get out. A group of well-dressed people head towards the open gates. When I'm sure they've gone inside, I hug the edge of the trees beside the cars to see if I can get a better look. There's clearly a party of sorts, and a lot of guests milling around with drinks in their hands. My eyes scan the pool area looking for Kirsten and Rodrigo. It's not long before they make an appearance outside the property; her first, pacing in black stilettos, a tight lilac dress hugging her curves and Rodrigo trailing behind.

'Come on, please. Don't be unreasonable,' he

pleads.

'Don't be unreasonable? That's bloody ironic coming from you.'

'I give you everything you want; the world is yours.'

'But you won't buy the yacht? What's a bloody yacht to you? It's pocket change.'

'It would only be for one night. What need would we have for it after that? We already have a yacht docked in Antibes. How about I rent one for the evening instead?'

'Rent one? What will people think? Our wedding's not important enough to you, is that it?'

'Of course, it is. You are everything to me.'

'Well, it doesn't seem that way. You don't care about me; you only care for yourself and your precious money.'

'That isn't true. You know that.'

'Do I? Selfish pig.'

She marches off, him chasing after her like a lost child. I stay perfectly still until they're completely out of view.

A cleaner clatters implements in the hallway. My breathing is laboured as I pull myself begrudgingly from the covers and check my phone on the bedside cabinet. A Facebook Messenger notification glares at me. I sit motionless, wondering who could be contacting me. I'd set up a fake account under the name of Graham Hartley, adding as many desperate random people I could call friends for more authentication. I'm relieved to see it is only spam, informing me I've been in a car accident recently and I have a right to a claim. The fact that I haven't only irritates me further, though it shouldn't. I've been bombarded by this kind of rubbish with my business, so it should come as no surprise. But the more garbage I'm buried under, the harder it is to dig myself out.

A new post from early this morning: 'Amazing Night with Amazing Friends. Thanks everyone :)'. I stare at the picture below: her and Rodrigo forcing a smile with their friends in the background. But it's one face that has the phone pinned to my hand. I pinch the screen and zoom in. Slightly looking away as if he's just realised the photo is being taken. Danny. I question what I'm seeing and rub my eyes, hoping they're deceiving me, but it's unmistakably him. I put the phone down and then look again, the shock sinking in as my brain desperately tries to figure out what the hell is going on.

He's in Bangkok, at least I thought he was. He's not said a single thing about coming to Chiang Mai or knowing exactly where she is. For all the trust I've allowed, it's now dissolving. He's screwed me over. How much has he told her? Does she know I'm here and why?

I roll through my contacts then stop at his name before I press Call. Let's see what he does or doesn't volunteer next time he rings me. Although I knew I was alone in all of this, I suddenly feel much more so. The room folds in around me and I reach for a glass, but think twice and drink straight from the bottle, slugging back as much as I can until I'm spilling it down my chin, onto my chest and pooling whiskey into the bed sheet. I stagger to the bureau where I try to prepare a joint. My hands shake to match the flickering flame from the lighter as I try to heat the hash. When I eventually stick the Rizlas, I light up, inhale, and sink back into bed, my mind spinning too fast to keep up.

The bottle is three quarters finished by the time I hear a knock at the door. I fall sideways and slam into the wall before I edge open the door to see Kasem's face peering in.

'Mr Ben, you okay?' He tilts his head to look beyond me.

'Kasem, not today, come back...' I slump into a heap, dribbling down myself like a baby. My trousers fill with urine as my bladder gives way. He pushes in with all his strength. He's there somewhere, but I barely notice him dragging me to the bed. I swing my hand out to grab the bottle.

'No Mr Ben, I no think you be needing any more of that.'

I'm laid down and I suddenly heave. He rushes over with the wastepaper bin as my shrivelled stomach erupts pure whiskey, missing the target. Toppling from the bed to the floor I lay there, sprawled in my own sea of sick.

My head is banging. Through squinted eyes I see elongated shadows on the wall and guess that it's late afternoon. I'm clean, the vomit is gone, and there at the end of the bed sits Kasem, his face waning a smile. He sweeps his hand across his already immaculate side parting.

'Ah, you awake, Mr Ben, good good. I order some coffee and then we talk.'

I try to form a protest but my mouth and throat are too dry and I only manage a strangled croak. He disappears, leaving me with shame as the barest of memories materialise of the morning.

The chink of cups draws me from a drowsiness I'm so desperate to keep. Kasem yanks me up and leans me against the pillows. My brain rocks against my skull from the light in the room, screaming at me from all angles to shut my eyes again.

'Please, may I be permitted to say that it is no good for you to drink like this?'

'No. You're just my driver.'

'Apologies sir, but you have me worried. It is dangerous for you to drink like that, and...' he prepares his skates for the wafer-thin ice, 'to smoke so much ganja too.'

'Listen, I pay you to drive, not to counsel me or be my doctor. I can just as easily get another driver. I didn't ask you to look after me, so shut up or leave.'

He smiles that same irritatingly calm smile, 'Yes sir, you employed me as driver, and today I come to drive you. But I no leave you like this. You choke, maybe nearly die if I leave you.'

'Maybe I want to. Maybe you're just being a selfish prick. And stop calling me Mister Ben. It's

Ben.'

'Okay, Mr Ben.'

'Not Mr Benn, the bloody cartoon character. Ben, alright... BEN.'

'Okay, Ben. I have order room service. A good pad Thai for us both. You will need to regain some strength if you wish to kill yourself.'

Food is the furthest thing from my mind. His kindness isn't something I'm used to, or maybe I just don't want to accept. He leans back in his chair, as if he knows something, a telling look he can see into the very heart of me. He lights one of my cigarettes without asking, ignoring the look of disgust on my face.

'We were all brought into life to learn from hardest of times,' he says, temporarily disappearing behind a plume of exhaled smoke. 'It is those times that show strength of character we become, how we adapt and how we handle situations. At end of darkest tunnel there is always light, and those who are enlightened by their plight are the ones who benefit most. Whatever you go through now will finish you or make you. It must be you and you only that make decision.'

He flicks the ash into the cup of his other hand, 'I do not believe you are bad person, despite your willingness to hate all around you. There are many bad people on this earth, but for every bad person there is also good. It's what you choose to see.'

I want to say something but can't be bothered. Instead, we eat, occasionally glancing at one another and I finish the meal with a ravenous hunger, something I've not had in a while. After another one of my cigarettes, he leaves, agreeing to pick me up later.

I can't bear the thought of going back to the villa. When Kasem returns, I ask to be taken into the city. I wander the streets, the shops and the stalls, glancing at the skilfully crafted ornaments and avoiding the hard sell. I hear traditional Thai music echoing the hall of an indoor market and step inside to see four beautiful young ladies in traditional Thai clothing, oranges and golds glittering and elegantly dancing, pointing toes and fingers in perfect unison to a small crowd of onlookers.

I haven't drunk alcohol or smoked since this morning. I'm in too much of a fragile state. My body feels as if it has nothing left to give, and I know the way I'm going, it won't be long before it gives out completely. Kasem's words resonate in me. I try not to listen, but they keep recurring to gain audience in the forefront of my thoughts. Silently I'm thankful, but I know it's not going to last.

Leaving the walls of the city to the lively bustle of the incoming night, I stroll over the reflecting lights of the canal and into a quieter street where I come upon a restaurant, semi-open to the road. It's quiet. I pass a girl with her back to me engrossed in a book on her tablet and sit a quarter of the way down, order a simple toasted cheese sandwich and a bottle of water. I relax and hope I can keep up this calm, this want for non-self-destruction and the anger that constantly rides me to stay at bay. But it crumbles as a group of three young American guys bowl boisterously into my space, one of them scraping his chair back against mine as they slam down at the table behind me. The girl who was quietly reading looks up at the commotion and registers my face. And I hers. It's the girl from the hotel in Bangkok, the attractive one. Amy, was it? She smiles and casually waves, but before I have the chance to return her gesture, the Americans take it that she's waving at them. They speak amongst themselves for a few seconds and having yet to order, decide to upheave themselves and barge their way into her space. They ask if the seats are taken around her, but before she answers, they sit down anyway.

Although I don't want to get involved, I can't help feeling concerned. She looks so frightened as they snatch away her tablet and pass it to each other in some immature game to gain her attention. I get up, enraged, but quickly restrain myself.

'Can't you see she just wants to be left alone?'

'What's it got to do with you, Jesus?' the stockier of the three says. 'The girl here wants to come back with us to our hotel.'

'I certainly do not,' Amy retorts and tries to stand, reaching out to retrieve her tablet and now her shoulder bag which they've grabbed from the back of her chair.

'Come on guys. Clearly, she's not interested.

Maybe try in the city if you want a bit of fun.' I put out my hand to hers. She takes it and I guide her away from the table. 'Would you return her things please?'

'You're starting to really annoy me, hobo.' He stands and closes in on me, the sour stench of stale beer on his breath.

'Look I don't want any trouble. Just give her things back and we'll be out of your way.'

For a second he looks away and then swings back with the tell-tale sign of a haymaker. I simultaneously block his forearm with my left hand and shift a heavy straight punch with my right square into his nose. He drops like an anchor to the table behind him.

His friends move in on me.

'Hey hey, no in here. No figh in here. You...' says the restaurant owner pointing at the Americans. 'You leave now.'

'But he started it,' one of them says like a child.

'I no care who star. You go now or I call police.'

They stand their ground for a few seconds, eyeballing me and then upend Amy's bag, the contents clattering on the table and rolling to the floor. Bloody Nose stares at me for a few seconds, gets to his feet and then spits at me. He turns and leaves with his companions, with one final sneer over his shoulder.

I offer an apology to the manager, hoping he'll allow us to stay.

'Okay, okay, no problem. Tae seat, I bring drinks.'

Amy makes herself comfortable at my table as a couple of Cokes arrive. She leans forward and places her hand on my arm, 'Thank you. I knew you were a good guy under all that grumpiness.' I go to say something, but her smile softens me. I can do nothing but close my mouth, dumbfounded by how beautiful she is in the light of her vulnerability. 'You really know your stuff. That was impressive.'

'Just luck. Anyway, where's your friend?'

'Oh, she's off with her new boyfriend. I'm completely forgotten about now, to the extent that I've been moved out of the hotel room we shared, and he's moved in. I'm staying in that place over there.' She points across the road to a cheap hotel with a blinking neon sign.

'So, you're on your own now? That must be tough.'

'It's not so bad. We hadn't been getting along ever since she's hooked up with Bentley.'

I nearly spit my drink out, 'Bentley? You're having me on?'

She laughs, 'Nope, cross my heart. Well, that's what he's told her, and she believes everything that comes out of that slick mouth of his.'

We continue talking for almost an hour. I divulge little about myself, minor details, such as my job and the town I live in in England. I try to divert her enquires by asking her about herself. The more she speaks, the more she reveals and the more I'm lost to her every word, falling into her, and drifting away from the events that brought me here in the first place. But when I least expect it, the photo from this morning leaps into my head and Danny's face clasps my cold attention.

I get up through her mid-sentence and say I must go. I pay the bill and as I'm about to leave, I look over my shoulder to the hurt in her eyes and a puzzlement spanned across her face. Rounding the corner by her hotel I walk for a few minutes and stop to light a cigarette. I hear a shuffle behind me, but before I have a chance to turn, I'm struck on the back of my head. I collapse to the floor and ball up to the onslaught of kicking to my face and torso. The excruciating pain of a boot in my lower back and stamp of a trainer to my ribs, another flurry of punching and kicking to my head before all becomes black and laughter dwindles to the curdling blood in my ears.

12

Once primary school was well under way, Emma and I would drive to Hythe and walk along the Royal Military Canal before her day started. She loved seeing the swans, especially the cygnets who rode upon their mother's back, and she'd always laugh at the cormorants diving and reappearing further down the canal with a wiggly eel in their mouth. We'd spot kingfishers occasionally and herons, and without fail we'd meet up with a retired lady called Mrs Twiss who walked Sadie, her black Labrador. Emma loved Mrs Twiss, who would always sneak a small packet of sweets into Emma's rucksack when I wasn't looking and raise her finger to her mouth as if it were their little secret. Of course, Mrs Twiss asked my permission, but that was between us.

Emma was ahead of us one spring morning

feeding the ducks when Mrs Twiss asked, 'So how are things with your lady friend?'

'Naomi? Good thanks. We're getting on well.'

'You've been seeing each other for a while, haven't you?'

'Yeah, I never thought I'd find anybody I could trust again, but she makes us both very happy and Isabelle gets on famously with Emma. I was considering asking Naomi to move in with us.'

'Oh, that's wonderful, Ben. You should, and maybe ask her to marry you too.'

I laughed, 'Slow down, one step at a time.'

'Well, you're not getting any younger, Ben. It's about time a good woman made a respectable man out of you.' She flashed a cheeky wink. 'And Emma, is she still enjoying school?'

'Can't get enough. It's such a lovely place to learn, the teachers are brilliant. She's coming along so well, and she's following in my footsteps. She's head over heels with art. She has a real eye for fashion too. When we're out shopping together, she tells me if she doesn't like what I picked off the rack for her and she'll point to something else instead. She even gives her opinion when I'm looking at clothes for myself.'

'Seems like you you've both got it all worked out then.'

'Do you know what, I think we have. We're a million miles away from where we were a few years ago.'

'That's wonderful, dear. Now where did Sadie

go?'

I thought about what she said and how we were now living our lives to the fullest. Every now and then I could see her mother in Emma, mainly in her stubbornness, but that would all dissolve when she smiled, and my heart filled with so much warmth. I couldn't love anyone more than I loved Emma. I held off asking Naomi to move in. We were happy where we were and at this stage, I didn't want to disrupt it all. I'd see how things went in the future.

For her sixth birthday, Danny surprised Emma with a trip to Disneyland. She was obsessed with the film *Frozen*. She couldn't believe it when Danny and I woke her early one morning and told her to get ready, and that we were off to Paris to see Anna and Elsa. I'm not sure who enjoyed the trip more, Danny or Emma. I'd never seen either of them so happy when they set sail on a musical boat ride through the magical world of Arendelle. Emma had fallen asleep in Danny's arms countless times when they were watching the film together, so it pleased him as much as me to see her face light up around every corner. We had a great photo together with the three of us posing with Anna and Elsa in their countryside cabin which was framed and placed next to Emma's bed.

Louise and Greg, not for want of trying, had been unable to conceive, so Emma made up for the child they longed for. Along with my parents, Danny, Naomi, and Isabelle, and even Mrs Twiss, we couldn't help but spoil her, but we were all keen to keep her feet on the ground, ensuring she understood the value of things in life. I knew from my own experience as a child that it wasn't what my parents bought me or where I lived, it was about the love they gave and knowing they would always be there for me, giving their support when I needed it the most. It was important to give Emma the same.

She spent Friday nights at my parents and Saturday nights with Greg and Louise. She loved helping Louise around the house, cooking and cleaning and earned some extra pocket money. She put it in her savings account, which she would sometimes dip into so she could be independent and buy her own books and toys. Danny couldn't help giving her a small gift every now and then, and despite me telling him not to, he paid money into her account every month for her future.

Emma was watching *Thomas and Friends* one afternoon with Danny when I received a phone call. Kirsten's voice spoke on the end of the line like a dark phantom from the past. She apologised for everything she'd put us through and said that she was desperate to be a part of Emma's life again. I was dumbfounded. Why now? Our lives were in such harmony. I didn't want any discord causing disruption.

Despite my reservations, it would have been wrong of me to deny a relationship between Emma and her mother, and after a lot of deliberation with Danny, Louise, and Greg, I agreed to a meeting on my terms. I wouldn't have Emma's life unsettled in any way. She was doing so well at school, 'A star student,' her teacher called her more than once. She had a pony called Anna that we kept in a paddock at the back of Greg and Louise's house which she adored, and she was becoming an incredible artist, constantly leaving me in awe of her talent. Her pictures were plastered throughout the house and on the studio walls. I couldn't let Kirsten destroy what we had worked so hard to become.

Seeing Kirsten for the first time in so long was disconcerting. Louise and I met with her without Emma so we could suss things out and discuss a way forward. I didn't tell Naomi. In truth, I didn't know how to. I didn't know what Kirsten's true intentions were or how it would all pan out. Either Kirsten had taken a course in acting or she was genuinely remorseful. She was calm and listened attentively to my terms, which included her never being alone with Emma, certainly not for the foreseeable future.

I had a long and difficult conversation with Emma. How do you tell a six-year-old about a mother that never cared for her? Of course, you don't. She was smart enough to fill in the blanks, and her soft innocent nature saw an opportunity to bond with the parent she never really knew.

Surprisingly Kirsten was great with Emma, and after three months, we let the reins off a little, allowing Kirsten to see her on a Saturday and Sunday with Louise temporarily supervising until we could be one hundred percent sure of our confidence in her. They took Emma shopping and for trips to the beach and even to Hever Castle and Chessington World of Adventures. But then the unreliability started to creep in. On several occasions Kirsten left Emma in tears when she didn't show up. She delivered a train of lame excuses, blaming unexpected work commitments, car troubles and other ridiculous stories. It was hard to see Emma this way, and I had to make some decisions to ensure her happiness. Either Kirsten committed one hundred percent, or she would never see her again. It was her choice. All or nothing.

13

I lick my parched swollen lips and clear the hoarseness from my throat. There isn't a single part of me that doesn't feel battered and bruised. I try to lift my arm, but it's constricted by a needle and tube. I'm propped up against a mound of pillows. Pain rings around my skull and I give up moving, too groggy with the effort. The dull light of the room competes with the darkness penetrating the gap in the curtains to my right. My other arm is held in a brace suspended a few inches above the blankets tucked tightly around my body. Sickness swirls through me and I feel like I'm about to black out. To my left, I make out a figure in the shadows, maybe a nurse, snoozing in a chair. My eyelids refuse the will to stay awake.

'Mr Ben?' I blink away the harshness of the sunlight,

flickering the image of a man leaning over me. 'Mr Ben? Kasem, remember?'

'Kasem.' I move a little and clear my throat, 'Where am I?'

'You in Ram Hospital. You are in bad way. You must take rest. No worry yourself, you are being looked after well here.' He drags a chair and sits beside me, 'Why you wanna play around like this?'

I groan as I try to adjust myself to ease the discomfort in my back, 'I don't even know what this is.'

'You got attack by group of men, much damage to you. Doctor say you have concussion, bruise spleen, three broken rib, shoulder dislocate, much bruising to legs and body also. And you have fat lips and nice big bumps on head and face. You look like a funny clown.' He chuckles, but I can tell it's only an attempt at making me smile by the look of concern in his eyes. 'You are lucky.'

'You call all of this lucky?'

'Oh yes. If lady not find you, could have been very bad. Much blood you lose.'

'What lady?'

'Lady who call ambulance for you. She make sure they know about your health insurance. All taken care of. She be here all the time with you. She even sleep here every night. I drive her back to hotel so she can rest a little. I watch over you now.'

'Do you know her name?'

'Oh yes, Mr Ben, very nice lady indeed.'

'Kasem, her name?'

'Oh yes. Miss Martindale. She say you are friends.'

'I don't know a Miss Martindale.'

'I have not spoke much with her, but she seem very fond of you, sir, very worried.'

'How long have I been here?'

'Three day.'

'What?' I jerk forward and yelp with a surge of pain.

'Stay still now.' He leans over to adjust my pillows and gently eases my shoulders into them. 'Now now, no rush.'

'I can't be here. Where's my phone?'

'In good time, Mr Ben. It is here in drawer next to you. No worry.'

'Stop with the Mr Ben shit. Seriously, I'd rather take another kicking than be called that again. Go and get me a whiskey.'

He laughs, 'Oh you are very funny Mr. Ben. NO.'

'No? I bloody pay you, don't I?'

Keeping his smile, he leans forward, 'No any more. Two days ago money run out. Tuesday today. Payment up until Sunday. I here as friend, only Lord Buddha knows why, but if anything, you are entertaining.'

'What? This is bloody entertainment for you?'

'Ah, that's the spirit, Mr Ben, good to see you have energy enough for colourful language.' He reaches behind him, pours a glass of lemon liquid, and brings it to my lips, 'Here, drink juice.' I take a sip, realising how thirsty I am, but trickle it down my beard in haste.

He mothers my chin with a serviette, 'Now I see you awake, I tell nurse and I go bring Miss Martindale to see you. She tell me to tell her if you wake.' He walks to the door, pauses, and turns back, 'I am very glad you are okay. Oh, by the way, I see Mr Benn on YouTube, very funny show.' He winks and leaves me exasperated.

An over polite nurse arrives shortly after, brings me sandwiches and tea, puffs up my pillows and confirms what Kasem had already told me. I will be able to walk and have the use of my arms, though very limited, and I will be in some discomfort for a few weeks to come. I'm strongly advised to take at least ten days rest to recuperate from my injuries and stay on the course of pain killers and antibiotics provided. I can be discharged tomorrow.

The time left alone to my thoughts is a blessing and a curse. I'm not feeling anxious about the attack. I felt it had done me some good. I'd been sailing far too close to the wind with my recklessness of late, not caring enough about myself nor the environment around me. I need to regain a grip on things.

Kasem left my phone on the bed, but I can't locate a wifi signal. There're a few missed calls from Kasem, one from Louise and two from Danny, plus four texts from him also. I ignore them for now. I can't deal with him on top of all of this. Instead, I stare out at the rooftops of the city from the window. Tomorrow can't come quick enough.

I must have dozed off. When I open my eyes again, the curtains are closed. In my peripheral I catch the glow of a small light. I turn around to find Amy sitting on the couch staring at her tablet. I'm not sure if I'm dreaming.

'What are you reading?'

'Oh Ben, you're awake. Robert Dinsdale's *Little Exiles*. How are you feeling?' she asks and places the device on the small table before her.

'What are you doing here? How did you know I was even in here?'

She walks over to the chair next me and plants herself down.

'I was the one who called the ambulance. You scared the life out of me. I thought they killed you.'

'You're Miss Martindale?'

'I am.'

'Listen, thanks and all, but this really isn't your problem. You can go now; you don't have to hang around.'

'I know.' She places her hand on mine and I instinctively move it away. She smiles, 'You've been through a lot, Ben.'

For a moment, I'm paranoid she knows more about me than she lets on and I glance around furtively for my phone. 'How did you know to call Kasem?'

'I checked your phone. Don't worry, I haven't looked at any of your personal stuff. I just checked your call history to see who you'd called most recently. Kasem's was a frequent number.' She leans forward and points to a rucksack on the floor, 'There's a change of clothes in there that I got from your hotel room. I had to tell the nurses that I was your girlfriend so they would let me have your hotel key.'

I nearly pulled the tube out of my bandaged arm as I shot forward, 'You've been in my room? You've got no right to do that. I can take care of myself.'

Despite my outburst, she stays calm, 'Yes, and I cleaned it up for you for when you return. Boy, you can drink and smoke,' she chuckles. I'm speechless with her supercilious tone. 'Look, I'm not one to judge. If you want to screw yourself up, that's your call, but if I'm being honest, Ben, I really like you. I've liked you since the first time I saw you in Bangkok, and despite your rudeness, I sense there's a good guy under there. I was hoping to see if I was right.'

I find I'm defenceless. Every time I want to get infuriated with her, I can't. 'You don't want to get tangled up in my shit. I'm not good to be around. My head is messed up at the moment and anyway I'm here on business, so I've got no time for pleasure or niceties. My advice to you, is to stay away.'

'Look, I'm not here to interfere with your life, but you must get some free time now and then, and when you do, I'd like to spend it with you, that's all. I was hoping I could pop in and see you while you rest at your hotel if that's not too much trouble.'

'I'm not planning on resting if I can help it, plus, I don't know how long I'll be in Chiang Mai, or

Thailand for that matter.'

'Well, I'm here for the next few days or so and then I was planning to head down to Phuket. You're welcome to come with me if you fancy a break.'

I say nothing. Her insistence to hang around me is kind of endearing, her presence magnetic, despite every part of me willing her to keep her distance.

Kasem collects my things, informing me on the way from leaving the hospital that the police still want to talk to me about the incident. I'm not inclined to speak with them. The further away from them, the better. As I am arriving at the hotel, my phone pings an SMS in my pocket. I take it out as Kasem leads the way up the stairs with my rucksack, me limping in tow. 'WHERE ARE YOU?' A pleasant welcome back to reality from Danny.

I pay Kasem for the last few days and the week ahead and ask him to leave me alone until the evening. I'm going to ask Amy out for dinner. I've been pretty good at screwing things up recently, so I can't see how one more thing is going to make that much difference. Anyway, it's the least I can do.

My room smells fresh and looks like a team of cleaners have been in, rather than just Amy. Everything shines and sparkles and the bed has been made perfectly, almost as if the pillowcases and sheets have been ironed. Why would anybody want to go to this much effort for me? Paranoia whips a dust storm around my chest, and with the reminder alert from Danny going off for a third time, I start to feel sick with the anxiety of where the hell my place on this earth is, if any.

I decide to phone Danny, get it over and done with, then I can return to my angst in silence. But as I hover over the call button, I think again. I really can't bear the sound of his voice, nor his condescending tone. I can't trust myself with what I know and how long I can cling to the fraying thread of his relationship with Kirsten. Instead, I text him, 'Misplaced my phone. Found it this morning. What's up?' Not that I really want to know, but I want an end to all of this. And Danny, I hope, is still the light at the end of the tunnel. Within minutes he's back to me, 'Be more careful. I need to know that I can contact you at a moment's notice. Kirsten is leaving for Phuket on Friday. She's staying at the Phuket Boat Lagoon, a marina near Phuket Town. I don't know exactly where, but I suggest you don't stay too close. Be in Phuket by Sunday.'

At least I don't have to wonder how he knows so much about her movements now, the snake. The nagging sensation that I'm being set up shivers through me again, but my curiosity of how this is going to play out is far stronger than me simply running away and hiding under a rock.

The pain squirming throughout me starts to grate, despite the double dose of painkillers I've thrown down my neck. I telephone reception, hoping one of the staff can run an errand for me to the 7-Eleven. A smiley teenager comes in after a gentle knock at the door. I tip him well when he returns ten minutes later with two bottles of whiskey in a brown paper bag. As he leaves, I ask him to ensure I'm not disturbed.

Leaning over and cursing at my aching ribs, I reach under the bed and rip away the tape holding the dwindling hashish strapped to the frame. Three skins, enough cigarettes to pack out a cigar sized joint, and a copious amount of pot should be plentiful to pull me below the undertow of the Mekhong river.

I look at my phone, debating to text Amy, finding the excuses of my absence for Louise, and stare at a smug photo of Kirsten on Instagram: 'Not long now until the BIG DAY :)'. The joint and a full glass stare back at me from the bedside table. I hate this merry go round. I want to be the me before her; the Ben I once knew, the Ben I respected but who's long gone.

Amy messages me back near enough straight away, 'I'd love dinner. Shall we meet at seven?' I reply and tell her I'll send Kasem to pick her up.

'Louise?'

'Oh, hi Ben.' She yawns, 'What time is it?'

'It'll be half six your end.'

'I'll wake Em for breakfast, she'd love to hear from you. Are you okay? I haven't heard from you for a while. Emma was beside herself.'

'Yeah, everything's fine. Just been busy with some clients.'

'Oh good, hold on.'

'Daddy, where were you?' Emma says, groggily.

'So sorry sweetheart, I got caught up with work,

but I'm here now.'

Silence.

'Emma? Are you mad at me?'

'I suppose not, but you said you would call really soon.'

'I know darling, I'm very sorry. What if I bring back lots of presents, will you forgive me then?'

'I just want you, daddy.'

'Oh, okay, I won't bring anything back but me then.'

'Maybe some presents will be okay.'

'All right then, darling. I'll go shopping before I come home and maybe I'll find some things in the airport too.'

'Can you buy me an aeroplane?'

'I might not be able to fit one of those in my luggage, they're awfully big you know.'

'Not a real one, a toy one, silly.'

'I'm sure I'll be able to manage that. So, are you going to school today?'

'Yeah, we're learning about insects. I have to draw spiders. I don't like drawing spiders.'

'Oh dear. Well, try your best, eh?'

'I will. Daddy?'

'Yes darling.'

'I had a dream about mummy last night.'

'Oh princess, are you alright?'

'Yeah, Aunty Louise looked after me. I woke up screaming. Mummy was so horrible to me. She was shouting at me and holding on to me really tightly. I couldn't get away from her.'

'It's okay now, eh? She's not going to hurt you, I promise. I'll be home soon to take care of you.'

'She scares me, Daddy.'

'Don't let her scare you. She's not around anymore.'

'Okay. I have to get ready for school and have my Rice Krispies now.'

'Snap, Crackle and Pop?'

'Ha-ha, yeah. Can we make Rice Krispie cakes again when you come back?'

'Of course, little one, I'd love that. Okay, you give Aunty Louise a big hug for me.'

'I will. Love you, Daddy.'

'I love you too, Emma. Take care.'

'I will. Do you want to talk to Aunty Louise again?'

'Yes please.'

'Okay, I'll go and get her. Bye Daddy.'

'Hi Ben.'

'Hey. How's she doing?'

'Oh, you know, missing you loads. She got really upset last night, but I managed to calm her down. We watched a bit of the Cartoon Network and I read her some stories.'

'Thanks so much, I can't tell you how much it means to me.'

'It's my pleasure, but try and wrap things up soon, eh? She's really missing you.'

'Of course.'

'I'm going to get her sorted for school now. Phone again soon.'

'I will.'

The noise from the street outside resumes and the click of the lighter on my skin brings me back to my reality. I lean back against the pillow, drink a full glass, and pour another.

A knock at the door makes me swear with the painful jolt that ricochets through me. I look over to the clock. 7.23pm. I pull myself up slowly, drain the dregs of the glass along with some crushed painkillers and call out to inform whoever is on the other side that the door is unlocked. Kasem breezes in.

'Ah Mr. B...' He clears his throat, 'Ben. I will take Miss Amy to a good restaurant. Maybe you could try and have shower, maybe some mouthwash and I will collect you in twenty-thirty minutes.'

'Thanks, Kasem.'

He smiles, almost sympathetically and leaves me until he comes back half an hour later. By then I've managed to clean myself up and pull myself together. I'm about to leave when the old guy from reception calls after me. He hands me an envelope with my name written on it. Inside is an airline ticket to Phuket. I suddenly feel sick. The reality of what I'm doing starts to sink in.

Amy's waiting patiently, browsing her phone when I walk gingerly through the doors of a cosy restaurant called EAT. The staff are at once attentive. She looks up as I sit down and frowns, 'How do you feel?'

I pad my face, feeling the ache of bruising,

'Getting there.'

A large bottle of water is placed on the table beside the menus.

'Thank you again for standing up for me with those thugs. Though I can't help thinking it's all my fault,' she says, reaching for a glass.

'What is?'

'Your attack. I mean, if I just handled them myself, you wouldn't be in this state.'

'You've got nothing to worry about. Anybody with a shred of decency would have done the same thing. Let's forget about it.'

As she scans the menu, I realise how serene I feel in her company. The tornado around me is silent, still ripping my world to pieces on the outside, but the equanimity she unconsciously creates within it allows me to breathe without suffocating. A comfortable moment of quiet passes between us before she says, 'Have you thought any more about joining me in Phuket?'

The chaos and solace collide.

'Um, I can try and meet you there.'

Her face lights up, 'Oh really? I honestly thought you would say no.'

I'm convinced she thinks I'm going there especially to be with her.

'I have some business to attend to.'

'Oh, but we can meet up though?'

'I'm sure I can find some time.'

'What sort of work are you doing in Phuket?'

'Just sourcing a location for a photo shoot for a

later date.' I divert her from probing any further, 'Kasem tells me you were in the hospital pretty much the whole time I was there.'

'Yes. I was really worried about you. There was so much blood, and you were unconscious when I found you. Kasem popped in every so often, but apart from that you were on your own.'

'Not much of a holiday for you.'

'It's not much a holiday spending it on my own anyway. Zoe is lost in Bentley land. I went to her hotel last night and they'd checked out. Can you believe it? She didn't even have the decency to tell me. God knows where she is now. She said she wanted to visit Chiang Rai, so I'm guessing they've gone there.'

'She sounds like a real charm.'

I'd got so caught up in this wonderland, I almost forgot what I could be implicating her in. If she's even seen to know me, it could open a whole world of trouble for her. I shouldn't be with her at all, but I can't seem to break myself away.

Aside from a Thai couple eating in the corner we have the restaurant to ourselves. We finish our meal; a khao phat kai for me, a dug-out pineapple with fried rice for her. Kasem chose this place well. I go to pay the bill, but she puts her hand on mine and insists, 'Please, it's the least I can do.'

Kasem is sitting in the car waiting for us. I open the back door, but she doesn't climb in.

'Do you fancy a walk, just for a little while and only if you're up to it?'

I lean into Kasem's window, 'Can you come back for me here in an hour or so?'

He looks to us both with a hint of a grin, 'Of course.'

Leaving the lights and sounds of the market stalls, bars, and restaurants behind, she takes my hand, 'Only to steady you,' she says. It crosses my mind to pull away, but I close my hand around hers and allow whatever this is to temporarily happen.

We stroll into the temple grounds of Wat Phra Singh. The only other visitor is a photographer with a camera propped upon a tripod. The place is teeming with tourists in the daytime, but the real magic appears to lie in the bed of night. An illuminated golden chedi sits alongside a glittering viharn with wing-shaped roofs, lavish wood carvings and stuccos.

An all too familiar sensation stirs in me. I suddenly pull my hand away from Amy's. I felt this before with Kirsten. For a second she seems confused but says nothing. She smiles and looks at me as if reading my thoughts, 'You can trust me, Ben. I'm not going to hurt you.'

I shy away, 'I should be getting back. I still have some work to do.'

Near Kasem's car, she pauses, 'Thank you for a lovely evening. Would you like to meet for lunch tomorrow?'

I try to summon up an excuse to say no, but instead I reply, 'I'll text you to let you know in the morning.' She steps forward, places a gentle kiss on my lips, but I stay rigid. She lets out a little laugh, more out of the embarrassment I think, and gets into the car.

'Kasem, could you come back to the hotel after dropping Amy off to discuss tomorrow please?'

When Kasem returns I ask him to take me straight to the villa.

'Are you sure that is wise sir? You should get some rest.'

'Kasem, just take me.'

I have no intention of entering the garden area of the villa. If I'm spotted, I'm in no fit state to make an escape. Instead, I quietly make my way up to a slight gap in the high fencing I noticed the first time I was here where I have a clear view of the property. The lights are on. Kirsten is pacing up and down behind one of the sofas between the kitchen and the living room. Classical music is playing, and although the doors are open, the music drowns out the detail of their conversation. He's holding his hands out in exasperation, maybe even pleading to her better nature. But he'll find none, that much I'm sure of. She stops to face him and leans forward to scream. He drops his shoulders, shakes his head from side to side and turns his back to her. She marches behind and pulls him round and slaps him hard across the face, enough to knock him back into the TV. He lurches forward and raises his hand into a fist. It looks as if she's coaxing him to hit her, but he drops his arm and leaves the room for the bedroom with her following closely behind. It's an all too familiar scene.

I hang around for another ten minutes with only Beethoven's *Für Elise* to keep me company. Kasem is busy watching a Muay Thai fight on his small TV attached to his dashboard when I get into the passenger seat.

Back in the room I pour a drink, whip back some painkillers, a xanax and a couple of tamizipans. The scales are weighed down so far on one side with Kirsten and shot high up on the other with Amy. I just need to blank my mind from it all.

The snatches of sleep I manage to catch only hold nightmares – Kirsten kicking and punching me from all angles, me helpless on the floor curled up enduring endless punishment. Sleep hasn't been easy for a long time. I'm not meant to be mixing my pills, especially with the quantities of alcohol I'm consuming, but the responsible side of me walked out of the door long ago.

With only a couple of hours to go until Kasem picks me up, I try to make myself half presentable considering the state of my face. I abandon the arm sling and clumsily start packing for tomorrow. I leave myself enough hash for today and a couple for the morning and throw the rest away.

The time is almost upon me and the prospect of what's about to happen sickens me in so many ways. I'm not a violent person. Yes, I've practised martial arts for several years, but that was purely for self-defence, and since school I'd never had the need to call upon it until I arrived in Thailand. I found an inner peace in Wing Chun, in both mind and body. But it wasn't enough, nowhere near enough. My mind has spent hours taunting me with Kirsten, replaying the endless splinters of our turbulent existence. My coping mechanisms have long been removed and every day is a struggle to keep it together. I'm on autopilot heading straight for the face of a mountain with all on board ready to go down with me.

Aside from Amy. I'll do all I can to protect her and keep her out of it as best as I can. She offers a composure I need to carry with me, and I'm starting to realise I can't do this without her. Although she knows nothing of what's going on, I need her normality and stability.

She waits at the cafe opposite her hotel. I didn't think anything of the rendezvous when I texted her earlier, but as soon as I arrive, a chill runs down my spine as the aching throughout my body re-enacts the scene from the alley.

She detects my discomfort, 'Shall we get away from here?'

Past the ruined walls, we cross the sparkling canal and head into the centre of the city where we laze in the shade of a coffee shop and order a sandwich.

'I'm leaving for Phuket tomorrow morning by the way.'

She reaches into her shoulder bag and slides the airline ticket across the table, 'Me too.'

'Um, we're on the same flight,' I notice.

'Really? Oh wow, that's a bit spooky. Maybe we might be able to swap seats and sit together.'

What she sees in me I cannot fathom. Apart from looking an absolute mess, I haven't been very nice to her so far and from what she must have seen of my hotel room, she surely knows I have problem with alcohol and drugs.

'Tell me about your family,' I say. 'Brothers or sisters?'

'I had a brother, but he died.' She glances away to a group of orange robed monks congregating on the street. 'You don't have to say anything. You're sorry, I know.'

'Were you close?'

'Very. He died of an aggressive malignant pharyngeal cancer. As soon as he was diagnosed, we knew it was the beginning of the end.'

'That must have been tough for you and your family. I mean, of course for your brother too, but to watch him go through that and know there was nothing you could do. I'm sorry, you probably don't want to talk about it.'

'It's okay. I've come to terms with it now. It still hurts thinking about it all, but you must go on somehow. That's what he said to me in his darkest moments, that I had to go on regardless and make a life for myself, to see things he would never see. And yes, all the while we went through it with him, it was very difficult.'

There's a momentary silence, and then she asks,

'And you, Ben, brothers or sisters?'

'A wonderful sister, Louise.'

I speak fondly of Louise and my parents, but I don't mention Emma. I like to keep her safe in my heart from anybody that I'm not over familiar with.

Once we leave the cafe we just walk, not really concentrating on where we're going. Weaving in and out of temples and finding respite from the burning sun in cafes takes us into the early evening. I can't believe things will change so dramatically in the next few days. As for now, it's as if the world is perfectly innocent with her by my side.

It's a strange feeling to have the malaise I've held as a partner for so long to take a back seat. It feels natural to enjoy her company, relax into it, basking in the light she shines. Moreover, the thought of Kirsten being miles away is enough to put me more at ease.

I bond with Amy over the news of her brother. I would never have known she suffered such a tragedy, and I cannot do anything but respect her courage and strength. I tell her as much as we sit on a wall with the deep scarlet of the setting sun shadowing the folds of the hills and stretching rice terraces beneath.

'You see a different side to me now,' she says, her eyes staying fixed on the horizon, 'but I was a wreck when we lost him. I went on a bender for six months, heavy drinking to dull the pain, not wishing to live anymore. I wanted to be with him so badly.'

I'm astonished. She seems so unharmed by life,

so together. When I first saw her in Bangkok, I would never have thought she was the girl by my side now.

'How did you straighten yourself out?'

'My parents. They found me passed out in their hallway one evening when they came home from a late dinner. I wasn't supposed to be there, but I'd run out of money and raided their drinks cabinet. It was the looks on their faces the following morning, the upset at the thought of losing their remaining child. Coupled with that, my promise to live my life to my brother solidified itself in that moment. I caught a glimpse of his face in the mirror. I'd seen the state of what I became because of his death. That wasn't living.

'It took me nearly a year of therapy and constant support from my family and friends. God knows how my parents managed to put up with me, but my counsellor said it gave them something to focus on. I really don't know where they got the strength from. One thing's for sure, I cope a lot better with life's upsets when I don't drink. I just had to believe it would all be okay, and it was. It's better to find a path to your dreams than live a life of wishful thinking. So instead of sitting around waiting for the answers, I started my journey here. What about you, Ben? What are your demons?'

'A mixture of things. One snowflake turned into a snowball and then into an avalanche. Now it's hard to dig myself out.'

She doesn't press for further information or offer words of advice; she just lets me be.

She kisses me on the cheek after dinner, and I offer her a lift to the airport in the morning. Despite my fears, I need her by my side.

I'm grateful of the rush from my first joint. I decide against a drink. I've become so immune to smoking pot now that I can almost function normally without it. When I hit the drink, and especially smoke at the same time, little makes any sense.

I roll back the years of my life, getting a little too sentimental along the way. I think of my mother and father, so very dear to my heart, who did nothing but support my dream of becoming a designer and photographer. If it wasn't for them, I would never have been the man I was once so proud of becoming. They invested so much time and energy in setting me up. They paid for my years at university, invested in my business. I paid them back once I started earning, but that isn't the point. It wasn't so much the financial backing, but more the encouragement they gave me, filling my life with positivity when I thought I couldn't make it countless times.

I think of my sister. Louise has never faltered at being anything but amazing and has consistently been there by my side. We've always had each other's backs. Being two years younger, I played the big brother on so many occasions, sticking up for her when she was bullied, being there to nurse her broken heart with boys. I'm so glad she discovered and married Greg. She couldn't have found a more perfect guy. Plus, she's been the mother figure Emma never really had.

Emma by far is the best thing that ever happened to me, and I miss her so much. She's with me wherever I go. However hard it is to hold them all in my heart, I will soon have to face the possibility of letting them go forever. But I can only accept this hurt at the very last moment, otherwise it will shatter me completely.

14

By now Naomi was aware of Kirsten's involvement in Emma's life and after Kirsten's constant set of failures to keep dates, she asked, 'Do you really think this is a good idea?'

'I must try, right? It wouldn't be fair on Emma if I didn't.'

'I know Ben, but she's not really making that much of an effort.'

She was right, but inside I had an overwhelming sense to protect Kirsten as well as Emma. Those same old emotions arose from the depths of all that was entombed, haunting me, and making no sense whatsoever. As soon as I saw Kirsten after so much time apart, my heart pined for her. And in a dream like state, I was drifting to her tune all over again, dropping everything at her every word.

It wasn't long before Naomi noticed something

wasn't right. I tried to push the feelings away, but I couldn't resist the hold Kirsten had over me. Every fibre in my soul told me it was wrong to allow her back into my head, but my heart ruled and threw out any reason.

I began seeing more of Kirsten and less of Naomi, all in hope we could be the perfect family I'd longed for. Naomi called it a day on a cold winter afternoon shortly after school. I was devastated that I'd hurt her and regretful of my decisions. We'd had so much in common and were great together. But pity the fool in hindsight, for as I was drawn to Kirsten once again, I realised nothing had changed. She was the same Kirsten she had always been, only this time, when she behaved the way she'd always done, and began cheating and lying again, it hurt all the more that I had been so stupid to let it happen.

After six months of living together, I asked her to leave. She was once again impossible to live with. This time I was stronger. I had to be, for Emma's sake, and where my little girl was concerned, I was calling the shots. Kirsten went crazy and smashed the house up, throwing whatever wasn't nailed down. Luckily Emma was at her grandparents. I said that I'd be placing Emma back on supervised visits for a while, and then she totally lost it. She stormed into Emma's bedroom and destroyed nearly everything. I couldn't believe it. I screamed at her to leave and eventually she did, breathing heavily like a rabid wolf. No tears, no remorse. Only venom in her wake.

I collected all the broken toys, the splintered wood and the ripped pages of Emma's books and sat with it all in the corner of her room in tears. It was only after several bangs that I came out of my daze and answered the door.

'Bloody hell, what happened here?' Danny asked, walking in.

While I was in a complete mess, he went about clearing up the house. He came and went throughout the day, leaving with everything Kirsten had destroyed and returning with boxes and more boxes. I hardly paid attention. I sat at the kitchen counter, hand on a vodka bottle.

When he'd finished, he told me to come upstairs. He opened the spare room, which was the largest bedroom, and told me to look inside. I was gobsmacked.

My parents brought Emma home to a house that looked as normal as it did when they left, only with a slight difference.

Danny whispered in my ear, 'Go ahead Ben, you tell her. It's all yours, mate.'

'Emma darling, can you go to your room for five minutes so I can have a chat with nanna and gramps?'

'Okay,' she sang, and skipped along the hallway. Danny put his hands up to keep silent before my mum asked what was going on.

'Um, daddy?' she called out, standing at her doorway.

'Yes, sweetheart.'

'Something's happened to my room.'

'Oh, what's that?'

'It's gone.'

'What? Don't be silly.'

I could see my dad's patience fraying, 'What's going on?' he said quietly.

I held up my finger and went over to Emma, 'What have you done to your room?'

There was only a bare single bed and her walk-in wardrobes.

She looked genuinely concerned, 'I haven't done anything.'

Her face fell and she began crying, tears dropping down her blouse.

'I'm sure we can work something out. Let's go and get you cleaned up, eh?'

By now she was inconsolable. It took several minutes to encourage her away from the doorway.

'All of my things are gone,' she wept.

'It's okay, petal.' I welled up as my parents looked on speechless.

Hand in hand, Emma and I went into the bathroom. I cleaned her sobbing face and told her to wait in the spare room.

'Whoa!' She spun round, her face a shock of awe and bewilderment. She turned back as if it were all a dream and screamed, 'DADDY!' and ran into her new room.

Inside was a fairy-tale kingdom fit for a princess, mostly running along a *Frozen* theme. There was a four-poster bed with pink ribbons twirled around the posts, *Frozen* bed sheets, pillows, and curtains. Brand new toys and games were lined up along one wall, all the characters from the film in their soft cuddly forms along another. She had a beautiful carved oak bookcase filled with books and an oak wardrobe to match. Hanging from the ceiling were seven bare lightbulbs, each a different colour of the rainbow. It was a little girl's dream. Tears rolled from my eyes as she hugged me tightly, 'Thank you so much, Daddy.'

I looked to Danny and mouthed, 'Thank you.'

Although at first Naomi and I didn't speak, the awkwardness at the school gates gradually subsided, but we would never be a couple again. We settled on good friends. For that I was truly thankful for. I didn't deserve it.

The business was thriving better than ever, and our client list was building by the month. We had to employ more staff to cope with the influx and opened another studio in London.

Emma and I spent our mornings walking our new English Springer Spaniel puppy, Elsa, along the canal on the way to school with Mrs Twiss and Sadie. We were safe, sound, and happy. We had risen from the ashes once more, but in the back of my mind, the presence of Kirsten's shadow was plaguing my thoughts more each day. I was determined to do everything in my power to ensure she wouldn't tear our world apart again.

15

The archipelagos, blackened by the shade of harsh sunlight, dot the approach to Phuket. Amy rests her hand on mine as we look from the window. She accepts what we have between us. I only wish I could offer her more. Conversation is brief. I'm not forthcoming and there's only so much space in the void she can fill. My mind is too cramped with thoughts failing my control.

A golden coast appears fringed with infinite palms clawing at the aircraft's wheels as we come in for a bumpy landing. I have no idea how far we are from the city centre, but I get a taxi without hesitation and lull in and out of sleep through the hour-long ride.

The hotel is candy themed: pastel-coloured stripes running along the floors, sweets in jars on the reception counter. I think it is Amy's way of bringing a little fun to our time in Phuket. She booked us two separate rooms in advance. A cloud bubble is painted on the wall above my double bed with the words, 'Sweet Moments, Make Memories'. In another lifetime, the designer in me would have loved it.

I meet her at her door. Behind her, I can see her room is decorated in the same pastel blue and white as mine, with a cloud bubble and a half-eaten cookie above her bed and the words, '...Are Made of Butter and Love'. I find myself smiling at her smiling, seemingly in love with the choice of accommodation.

She points at a poster on the wall as we sip coffee in the hotel's restaurant, 'There's a food festival nearby in the Indy market tonight,'

'Should be good,' I reply, although I'm not sure I look convinced. I try to keep above the swell of black water, for her sake and to an extent mine.

A text alert flashes on my phone. I slide open to read a message from Danny, 'Meet me at Komkai's Cafe, Old Phuket in one hour.' Amy's face drops as I tell her I must leave. I promise I'll be back by six. As always, she accommodates me.

Along the strip of coloured Sino-Portuguese buildings of Thalang Road I search until I find Komkai's. Apart from a young Thai guy wiping down tables, the place is empty. I ask if he's seen a guy called Danny and he nods towards a stairwell. At the back of another room stacked with chairs is an office with Staff Only written on the door. Danny sits behind a desk leafing through paperwork.

'So, this place is yours as well?'

He takes two beers from a refrigerator behind him, 'Mine and my cousin's. Shut the door.' He uncaps both bottles and hands one to me, 'You're looking good, Ben.'

I bypass the sarcasm and finally confront him with my knowledge, 'So what's the deal with you and Kirsten?'

'What?'

'Don't play dumb, Danny. We've known each other far too long. You were in Chiang Mai with her.'

'Oh right, how did you find out?'

'Through the power of Facebook.'

'You met my uncle then?'

'Who?'

'Kasem.'

'Okay, that makes sense. He's sneaky for keeping that quiet.'

'I needed someone to look after you, mate. Clearly by the amount of alcohol you've been consuming, not to mention getting your head kicked in, you weren't doing a very good job of it by yourself.'

'Well, Kirsten?'

'I had to keep tabs on her, know her every movement.' He opens a drawer in his desk, pulls out a stainless steel and black finished handgun and changes the subject, 'Browning 1911 380 Black Label Pro .380 ACP Semi Auto.' He tilts it from side to side, 'Holds eight rounds, has an extended ambidextrous thumb safety. It's extremely powerful at close range.'

It looks like a toy until I feel the weight of it in my hands. It then becomes very real.

'You remember what I told you and how to fire one?' How could I forget? A cold and wet evening in Dungeness shooting at cans on the desolate beach. Almost an identical looking gun. I nod, shrinking at how dangerous Danny really is and how he knows his weapons so well. He takes it back from me. 'You can pick it up tomorrow evening. We'll go through the final details then. The wedding ceremony is taking place on Maya Beach by the way.'

I raise my eyebrows, 'Unbelievable!'

'Uh huh. Rodrigo has bought off all the tour companies that go there and paid a hefty sum to hire out the entire island for the morning. Nothing is a problem for his princess. The guy is loaded, Ben, I mean absolutely rolling in it. The reception is being held on an Astondoa 110 Century superyacht docked in the lagoon. He bought it solely for the occasion. They're also using it to sail out for their honeymoon around the Gulf of Thailand.'

'He gave into her whining then?'

'Sorry?'

'Nothing. How comes you're so close to her suddenly? She hates you.'

'I had to befriend her. I said I fell out with you. How else do you think you're going to get anywhere near her? He's got security posted everywhere. Even when they appear to be on their own, he's got his goons close by somewhere. He's had several attempts on his life already. You don't get that rich without pissing a few people off. I needed to win her trust so when the time comes, everything runs smoothly. This is why you're in Thailand remember? With the amount of time passed since you last saw her and the fact that nobody would ever suspect you're here, it should all pull off smoothly. All you need to do is focus on the day after tomorrow.'

'So how is this all going to go down?'

'I'll let you know when we meet here again. Not until then. I don't want to give you too much to think about.' He leans forward as I stand, 'I'm only going to ask you one last time, are you sure you want to go through with this?'

I'm aware that every second is another moment to change the outcome of my life. Each choice I make is mine alone, deciding a different alternative of my future, but I've waited too long.

I get up and open the door, 'More than ever.'

Amy shouts out she'll be there in a minute. Her hair is wet, and she is wrapped in a towel when she finally appears in the doorway, 'Sorry, I've just got out of the shower. Take a seat, I'll be with you in a minute.' She goes into the bathroom and calls out over a hairdryer, 'Did you get everything sorted out you wanted to?'

'Yes thanks. What did you get up to?'

'I met Zoe briefly. Trouble in paradise apparently. Suddenly I'm her best friend again when it comes to

Bentley screwing her around.'

'Ah right. She's in Phuket then?'

'Yes. Somehow, she found out I was coming down here. I told her I didn't have time to hang about and cut the conversation short.'

'Did you say anything about me?'

'No. I guessed you would want it that way.'

'Thanks.'

We head out for the short walk around the corner to the Indy Market. Stalls waft out various spices from a variety of freshly prepared Asian food. We share some shumai – steamed shrimp and pork dumplings – while watching a girl singing over an acoustic guitar. We're the only westerners around and it feels good to be free of the threat of tacky tourism at our heals. We move on to the Old Phuket Coffee Station in the old town.

Amy looks up from her cappuccino, 'You seem a little distracted, even more so than usual.'

'I've just got a lot on my mind.'

'You can always talk to me, you know.' She reaches over and gently puts her hand on my arm, smiles, then leans back, 'Well, if you're not doing anything tomorrow, I've taken the liberty of booking us a tour out to the Phi Phi islands. What do you say?' I can tell she's preparing herself for a no, but her eyes light up when I agree. 'Oh really? That's great. One of the places we'll visit is Maya Bay where The Beach was filmed. Have you heard of it?'

'Um, yeah.'

'I read the book a couple of months ago and

loved it. I wasn't overly struck on the film though. Not that I'm saying it was all bad, I'm just not so much into book-to-film adaptations.'

'I loved the book.'

'Really? You read it too. I thought it was such a shame they cut Jed from the film.'

'He was my favourite character next to Richard and Keaty.' I paused and then asked. 'You don't know somebody called Danny Komkai do you?'

She thought for a moment, 'I knew a Daniel Taylor once. But that was years ago. Why do you ask?'

'No reason'

I spent most of the night drinking after kissing Amy goodnight at her door. I feel terrible by the time I meet her in reception. I have on a pair of sunglasses to hide the bloody roadmaps in my eyes. She looks amazing, even through the fog and raging headache. We rush through a greasy breakfast before setting off in a car sent by the tour company. The driver is a young guy, very chatty. Amy converses with him effortlessly. I hardly say a word as she holds my hand tightly all the way. In the very last moments of who I am, I am falling helplessly in love with her. It's making things so much more difficult.

When we turn into the Marina, I nearly choke as I see a sign for Phuket Boat Lagoon. I had no idea we were starting our day from here. If I had, I would never have come. The last thing I need is Kirsten to see me.

Amy picks up on my paranoia straight away, 'Are you okay?'

'Yeah. Fine,' I snap.

We're led into a room, where along with some other tourists, we're given a safety briefing by a friendly Thai who's leading the tour. He says we can call him Tom Cruise, making everyone laugh. Already I feel uncomfortable with these other people hemmed into a boat where I can hardly breathe, mind about stretch my legs. Suddenly the thought of being back in my hotel room with a supply of alcohol becomes ever more tempting.

Perched at the end of the boat, I stare out over the engines to the glittering azure waters and white pencil lines of the Andaman beaches. Every so often islands appear abundant with foliage, some far too small to inhabit humans, some just big enough for an isolated house or two. Amy smiles occasionally, as if to read my restless thoughts. I'd love to let her in, if only I could.

The announcement of Maya Bay echoes over the loudspeaker as we turn into the cove, the colossus of jagged rocks dwarfing all boats passing beneath. The magic of when Alex Garland's characters, Richard, Françoise, and Étienne, first set eyes on the beach is all but lost to the hordes of tourists that overrun the golden sands. Amy, like me, is dismayed by the noise, litter, and sheer amount of people as we navigate our way around the GoPros on selfie sticks and cheesy grins. I think our guide has registered our faces. While the other passengers of our boat are at one with their surroundings, he approaches us and guides us away to a discrete spot uphill where passers-by are oblivious of our whereabouts.

He lands his hand on my good shoulder, 'No many people know of this little place.' He coaxes Amy to take a picture, 'Stay for a time here and enjoy the view. I call for you later.' He joins the rest of the group to take care of their needs.

'It is beautiful, but not quite what I expected,' Amy remarks as she removes a cigarette butt from between her toes. 'It's a bit packed.'

'It's nice to see it all the same.' I fade out for a moment thinking of tomorrow morning and the wedding that will take place right where I'm looking.

Tom Cruise waves over in our direction and ushers us away twenty minutes later. How ironic this idyllic setting has become everything the travellers of Garland's novel were so desperate to escape.

The boat backs out of the crystal turquoise waters and stops for a while for those wishing to snorkel and see the multi-coloured marine life. Amy and I hang back, indulging the peace while the others dive near the limestone cliffs of Tham Phaya Nak, also known as the Viking Cave. Tom tells us the bamboo scaffolding braced around the mouth of the cave is constructed by hunters who seek out edible swiftlet's nests. Prized in Chinese culture, the nests are believed to promote good health. The hunters climb under the cover of the night to carry out this risky, but well-paid job.

The tour takes us on to the cove of Ao Ling, home to a colony of monkeys scurrying around alcoves or screeching from vines. They eye up the chance sightings of food and a few of the more confident ones climb aboard to the gaping mouths of the onlookers at the front. Just after midday we're awarded the almost deserted golden sands of Laem Thong where we wade out to the shallow banks passing a few longtail boats moored along the way. A restaurant serves a buffet lunch which I avoid, heading instead for a bottle of Fanta. Amy browses the fruit aisle. When she arrives at the table, I ask her if she really wants to eat the slice of watermelon on her plate. 'I'm sure it'll be fine,' she says as she cuts into it.

'I'm not,' I reply, and point to the tiny maggot crawling from the side.

She drops it in disgust, 'Ewww.'

I laugh, 'I'll shout you some dinner later.'

With some time left, we wander the long stretch of beach and take advantage of the shade under the palms hanging over the sand.

'I've only got tomorrow before I have to head back to Bangkok,' she says.

I gaze at a hermit crab lazily moving past us. 'How long are you staying in Bangkok?'

'Two days and then I fly home. How about you? Are you staying in Phuket?'

'I think so, for a while at least.' I have no idea what the future holds.

'Well, if you can get a flight, you can always meet me in Bangkok.'

She checks for a reaction and looks out to the sea when she sees none.

After another hour on another beach staring out at a horizon of jagged islands, we leave under an increasingly menacing sky. My phone vibrates as we dock into the marina. 'Komkai's – 7pm tomorrow.' My heart sinks at the thought of Amy and I coming to an end, of the possibility of a life I could never have imagined being taken out of my hands. I watch her as she searches through the seashell framed photos, looking for the one of us, taken at the beginning of the tour.

'What do you think?' she says, breaking me away from my pensiveness. She holds up the picture and laughs, 'You look great, but I closed my eyes when the flash went off.' She tucks it into her holdall, 'We look good together though, eh?' She nudges me playfully.

The storm reaches the town and veins of lightning strike through the puffy clouds of the night sky. We shelter from the hammering rain in a restaurant filled with young locals; old fashioned radios and TV sets stacked along the walls. Deep bowls arrive at our table filled with colour: yellow noodles fried with eggs, succulent shrimp stir fried with tamarind sauce, braised pork in a rich pepper sauce, a curry of sweet crab in coconut milk with wild betel leaves and thin rice vermicelli noodles.

Something different with each mouthful alighting our senses.

Back at the hotel, Amy asks me in for a coffee. I agree and tell her I'll join her after a quick shower. From my balcony under the light of the full moon peeking through the ribs of broken cloud I lose myself to this bewilderment; of falling in love and being filled with so much hate. I can't figure out which is winning as the two battle to take centre stage – excited butterflies grasped by fists of anger.

I push the door open to Amy's room, but she's curled up asleep on the bed. I pull the sheet over her, switch off the lights and leave her to her dreams, returning to the cold comfort and familiarity of my intoxicated mayhem.

Laying on the bed, I scroll through pictures of Emma on my phone. I need the distraction but my vision doubles and blurs. Instead, I scroll down my list of contacts.

'Hello? Louise? Have I told you how much of an amazing sister you are?'

'Ben, have you been drinking?'

'Maybe. But have I told you?

'You have. How are you?'

'I'm okay. I miss you, but I miss Emma more. Put her on the phone.'

'I don't think you should really be talking to her like this.'

'Ah come on, I've waited all day. I miss her.'

'She misses you too. But Ben?'

'Oh please.'

'Okay, but only for a short while. Don't let her know you've been drinking.'

'Of course not. Louise?'

'Yes.'

'Am I a good father?'

'Yes Ben. Now let me go and get her for you and be quick, eh?'

'I will. I love you, Louise.'

'You too. Emma, it's your dad on the phone.'

'Daddy?'

'Hello, my beautiful girl, how are you? What have you been doing? Tell me everything.'

'I got a good mark for my insect drawings today. The teacher really liked them and put one of the pictures up on the star board near the headmaster's office.'

'Oh Emma, I'm so proud of you. I knew you could do it. You've got so much talent; you truly are amazing. Wow, the star board, that's because you're such a star.'

'You sound funny, Daddy.'

'I'm fine, precious. I'm just really pleased for you. What else have you been doing?'

'I rode Anna after school and nearly came off.'

'Oh my God. Are you okay?'

'Yeah, I'm fine. It was scary though. Aunty Louise was with me luckily.'

'Oh okay. Are you sure you want to keep riding?'

'Of course, I love it.'

'And I love you, so much that my heart is fit to burst.'

'You're so funny, Daddy. What's wrong with your voice?'

'Oh nothing, I just have a bit of a toothache that's all.'

'Are you coming home now?'

'Soon, I promise. I must go now, darling, I'm sorry.'

'Don't be sorry, Daddy, just come home.'

'I will. I'm right by your side, always.'

'I love you, Daddy.'

'I love you so much too, little lamb.'

The warm sun latches on to my skin, steadily rising from its hearth and beaming through the open window. A tap is running, and the place is a state. An odour of spirits and stale smoke haunts the air. I struggle forward and see an oak-coloured puddle at the end of an empty bottle on the floor, beside it a half empty glass of vodka and a bottle of Mekhong still sealed. I wipe the crust of sleep from my eyes and edge towards the bathroom, sluice my mouth with the water from the running tap and wash my face and matted beard with the complimentary soap. My chest burns painfully, my throat feels fierce, the inability to swallow inhibited by the lack of saliva.

Every night I'm captured in dreams of violence, helpless to those who feed from my fear, baring teeth gritted with pleasure at my pathetic demise. I take sleeping pills in hope I blank out the night, waiting to wake in the morning to my own pitiful whimpers and my clinging cold sweats. Another day will cast its long shadows, the sun will laugh at the moon's smug arrival and the torturous ticking of the clock will once again drag me towards oblivion.

Last night I dreamt nothing. For the first time in months, nothing. I wrestle to piece together what happened after I left Amy's room. I try to force upon me the hours lost. Aside from slugging from a bottle, nothing materialises. The only evidence is the disregard for my existence scattered around me and the panic of my failing mind. Very little in life makes sense or has purpose anymore. Passing through this emotional theatre, Emma is all that forges the little clarity I have. More and more of me decays, all my recollections a struggle to manage. The ghosts that appear as throttled memories are merely the last time I remember them – a copy of a copy – weakening by the day.

I combat my thirst and stinging hangover with a large glass of vodka, smoke a couple of cigarettes and stumble with the rush into the shower, bottle in hand. The water washes over me but does nothing to cleanse my despicable soul. The past reaches forward and meets with the present, folding alternatives of the evening ahead. I thought when this day would arrive, I'd be thwart with nerves, but it comes only as a relief as I vicariously play out Kirsten's reaction upon seeing me, begging for her life in my hands.

Over coffee I glance at Amy as the light falls upon her flawless skin. She wears her hair in a ponytail, her eyes igniting when she looks at me and I offer what I can in the way of a smile. We stroll along market streets, past snoozing stall holders hidden behind trays of fruit and vegetables, look away from the chopping boards of the meat markets and follow the floral essence of the flower stalls to watch ladies sewing orange and yellow flowers into garlands. We stop for tea in a cafe and eavesdrop on travellers' tales while gazing at cops directing unruly traffic: kids staring out from the windows of school buses, trucks packed with workers dismayed at the long slog ahead, motorbikes piled with two, three or families of four.

We weave in and out of the Jui Tui Shrine and Put Jaw Chinese Temple where I'm happy to take a back seat with my thoughts as Amy photographs the red coin tiled roofs, decorative steps to the altars, the dominating stone statues of gods and dragons and the dozens of statuettes that line the dusty shelves in the many halls. She pauses in respect of the worshippers kneeling, holding aloft incense in prayer to a bronze bowl, dragons each side with a blazing fire at the centre.

She is well rehearsed for our day, hailing a cab, taking us up into the fertile hills to Wat Khao Rang. Dominated by a giant golden seated Buddha, the temple has a sloped roof of red and gold with eerie statues carved into the walls. Adorning the inner walls are images that soak the interior with a depth of colour, depicting stories of the life of Lord Buddha.

'Ben, did you not see the snake?' Amy says, startled as we leave.

'What snake?' I reply.

She points behind me at a vibrant green serpent coiled and bobbing, 'You just walked right over it!' I step back to let it glide gracefully down the hill and into the cover of the ferns.

A taxi drops off a Thai couple and Amy flags the driver to take us to the other side of the island and to the summit of the Nakkerd Hills. We disembark to the 45-metre-tall Big Buddha, constructed with reinforced concrete, and layered with Burmese white marble. For a while we silently look out to the sweeping vistas of the island and the sea. I take both her hands in mine, look deep into her eyes, 'I've known you for so little time and yet it feels like forever. If I were in a different place, I promise you...'

She stops me by placing her finger to my lips, the precipice she clings to all but crumbles away, 'No buts, no ifs, let's simply exist in the moment.'

Tears form in her eyes. She turns away and looks downwards to the town, knowing in her heart that this will be the last time she'll ever see me.

I walk her slowly to the waiting taxi, kissing her gently and turn to leave. I dare a glance back to see if the car is gone but find her running towards me. She embraces me so I can hardly breathe and rests her head upon my shoulder, 'Please take care, Ben.'

Danny is talking to a member of staff as I near his

office. He sends him away when he sees me and invites me to sit opposite. He relights a cigar from an ashtray on the desk and blows a thick plume above my head.

'Bloody hell, your ex is a nightmare.'

'Good day?' I ask, waving away the smoke.

'A bride couldn't ask for more. A superyacht takes her and her guests to a secluded piece of paradise for a dream wedding and all she can do is moan the whole time about how this wasn't perfect or how that wasn't good enough. Rodrigo has had teams of people working around the clock to make sure everything runs smoothly. But oh no, she has to find something that didn't quite live up to her ridiculous expectations. How the hell did you put up with her for so long?'

'I have no idea.'

'How she has you lot rolling over like puppies, I'll never know. Anyway, down to business.' He slips a folded piece of paper before me, opens it to a hand drawn diagram, 'This is a map of the Boat Lagoon.' He points behind a row of badly scrawled boats to what looks like a jetty of sorts, 'I want you here in this blind spot, between these two buildings. Darkness is your best friend. She'll come out at eight and walk to the shopping mall which is here. When she comes back, step out of hiding and do what needs to be done.' He reaches behind him and lifts a brown paper parcel from the top of the fridge, 'Inside this is a pair of black jogging bottoms and a hoody with large enough pockets at the front to conceal the gun. Make sure you aim where I told you and then get out of there as quickly as possible.' He slides his finger along a pathway on the illustration, 'Follow this path from the Lagoon. Out in the street a car will take you straight to the airport. Leave the gun in the vehicle and board the private jet that will be waiting for you.'

'How do you know she's coming out at eight?'

'Because she's been snorting coke all day and drinking. She'll get a taste for the weed I've got stashed when I open it up under her nose. That much I'm sure about. I'm going to send her to get some rolling papers which the supermarket doesn't stock. She won't want to smoke anywhere near the yacht. Rodrigo hates the stuff and she'll not want to alert any of the staff either.' He stubs out his cigar and swipes the smoke between us. 'If anything changes, I'll text you. Make sure you keep your phone on vibrate. Study this map and when you're there be careful and for Christ's sake, don't panic.' He folds the paper back in two. 'Don't drink or smoke anything before you leave. Do not brush your teeth or wear aftershave and don't smoke while you're at the marina. Strong scents can be detected at distance. Kasem will be at Komkai's at 7pm to take you to the Lagoon and he'll be waiting outside to take you to the airport.'

'Kasem?'

'Next to you, he's the most trusted person I know.' He leans forward and looks the most serious I've seen him since he spoke about his time in the regiment, 'This is going to be a lot more difficult than you think. All sorts of stuff will run through your head at the very last second before you pull the trigger. If you want to step away from this, do it now, because if you screw up, you're in for a lengthy sentence sharing a cell with a bunch of lunatics waiting for the firing squad.'

I look him straight in the eye, 'Danny, I want to do this. This is the only way to stop her. If anything does go wrong, I'll turn the gun on myself.'

'Stick to the plan diligently and it won't come to that. Pack all your stuff, bring it with you and leave it here. Be here early. Grab a green tea or something and take a breather. This will be the last time you'll see me for a while. I'm going back to the boat to keep on top of everything.'

He gets up and comes around the desk as I rise, 'Thank you. For everything. I don't know how to repay you,' I say.

He bypasses my outstretched hand and pulls me into a tight hug, 'You're my brother, Ben. You've always looked out for me, there's nothing to repay.'

I creep past Amy's door at the hotel. She's got plans to meet Zoe at four for dinner, so it's doubtful she'll be in. There's no question I'll miss her. Her smile alone rose me from the depths of my depravity and silenced the gaping void of endless voices while I was with her.

I pack my stuff quietly and ensure the room is spotless and sit on the bed tapping my foot impatiently for 6pm to arrive, scrolling through post after post on social media of the newlyweds.

I take one final look at myself in the mirror. The bruise around my eye is still angry, but the swelling has receded. My lips are normal again, aside from a deep reddish split on the right. Although my body is still wracked with pain, it's manageable. It keeps me alert. I inhale deeply and leave.

Sipping from a bottle of water, I glance around Komkai's at the handful of locals and tourists. It was so easy to think I'd have a calm confidence about me. Now, the escalating nerves and paranoia are taunting, making me uncomfortable and twitchy. I sit by the window staring out at the illuminated blue residence opposite, desperate for this to be over with.

I'm at the edge of my seat when Kasem appears at the doorway and nods in my direction. I follow him in silence along the street and around a corner where a goods truck is parked. I'm about to climb into the passenger seat, but he guides me around the back. Coloured plastic trays are stacked to the top. He reaches into one on the far left and I hear a latch click to reveal that the trays are a facade acting as a hidden door. It's hard to read him as he gestures for me to get into the empty space. He closes the door behind me. I hear the turn of the ignition and engine rumble to life.

Half an hour elapses by the time we come to a permanent stop. As he opens the door, a small shred of light floods the interior. I hold my finger up for him to wait as I study the map a final time. Stepping down, I thank him by placing my hand on his shoulder. He looks around and unwraps the gun from a white towel. I slide it into my front pocket, lift my hood and slink away along the path into the marina.

For moment I'm sure I've taken a wrong turn, but then I see the tip of the illuminated lighthouse on one side of the harbour, the shopping precinct on the other. Under the bare light of the moon, I continue until I find the jetty, and guess by the thump of Drake's Hotline Bling, I'm within proximity to the yacht. I slip into the shadows between two wooden storehouses, check my watch and wait for the fifteen minutes to elapse.

My chest smoulders with the uncertainty of being face to face with her again and what I'm about to do. Suddenly I hear voices coming closer. I crouch down and pray I'm not seen. Inches away, Rodrigo and Kirsten stop, desperate for each other to be heard over the music in the background.

'Send one of the staff, Kirsten. Come back to the party,' he deplores.

She breaks away from him, 'I need to get some fresh air and be on my own for a while, away from all the noise.'

He looks on as she saunters away and then returns the way he came.

I should do it now, go after her and get it over and done with, but my feet stay pinned to the ground. I know Danny will be wondering what's going on, probably waiting for all hell to break loose when someone finds her body. But that's his problem now. I need to concentrate and get it together for when she returns.

After twenty minutes she still hasn't come back. I try to catch a glimpse of her and as I shift forward, I step right into her path. It takes me aback as much as it does her as she lets out a small yelp in surprise.

'Excuse me,' she says, not recognising me behind the beard, eyes shaded by the hoody. She sidesteps me and I mirror her actions. She stands still for a moment feigning confidence in her sleek black dress and high heels. She looks up, directly at me, frustrated, worried even, and then it registers.

'Ben?'

'Kirsten.' I squeeze the grip and circle my forefinger around the trigger.

She backs up slightly and looks over my shoulder, 'What are doing here?'

'I can't believe you've actually married this one.'

'We're in love.'

I once adored that surreptitious smile but came to realise it was nothing but sly and condescending.

'Oh really?' I laugh, the sarcasm sliding from my lips. 'Since when have you loved anybody but yourself?'

'I stand to gain a lot.' Despite her confidence, she starts to shake, 'Move out of the way, Ben.'

She sidesteps again, as do I, 'You've wrecked mine and Emma's world.'

'Look at the state of you. You've done a fine job

of that all by yourself. And I'm sick and tired of hearing about Emma. Now get out of the way or I'll call security.'

All restraint topples. I pull the trigger, but it sticks. For Christ's sake. I tentatively fiddle with the safety, trying to stop myself shaking as I stall for time.

'So, you're nice and cosy with Danny?'

She chuckles, 'You know he's here then? He told me he hasn't spoken to you in ages. He and I are quite the item. We've been together for over six months now behind Rodrigo's back. Did he tell you that? Oh, judging by your face, I guess that's a no?'

I clip the safety back into place, heeding to caution that I'm being set up after all.

She looks over my shoulder again, 'Run along Ben, you wouldn't want things to turn nasty. He's armed.'

I risk a glance. A well-built guy in a black suit wanders towards us.

She puts her hands on her hips and smiles smugly. Defeated, I weigh up my options: kill her or be killed or exchange all of this for an execution squad. Any courage left suddenly abandons me. I decide instead to sprint.

I keep running until I make it to the exit and scan the parked vehicles for any signs of the truck. A few cars down I see it peeking out from a side road. I'm left with the decision of whether to go it alone or trust Kasem. I take my chances, turn right, and jump into the back. A pale blue shirt, a pair of jeans and trainers are stuffed into a plastic bag along with an envelope holding my passport and wallet. A note says, Leave Mr Browning with the hoodie and joggers.

By the time we reach the airport, I'm still none the wiser of Danny's motives.

16

Pelting rain drenched me as soon as I stepped out from Hong Kong International Airport to a line of red taxis. Draped over the hills, thick clouds blotted any views and the sheets of water they disbursed reduced visibility to a bare minimum. The ancient windscreen wipers whined and struggled to keep up with the torrent. Coupled with the hair-raising driving, I dreaded the prospect of not making it to the hotel at all. The sky was gunmetal and vicious by the time I did arrive, all the shop signs were a circus of colour spattering reflections on to the streets, despite it being 7am. I checked in and went straight out. The last thing I wanted was to be holed up in the hotel waiting for the rain to ease. I didn't have the time. I was on such a tight deadline and had so much to do. I'd start in Mong Kok where my hotel was situated and work my way around the city from there.

There were few people on the streets. An occasional collection of walking umbrellas, but other than that, for a short time at least, I had the area in relative peace. I began by taking photos of the long avenues and multi-story buildings soaring into the mist. It was a challenge just to keep the camera dry and I was soaked within minutes, but the ideas flowed as I envisaged the perfect shot. It was hard not to stop and stare at the weather-stained apartments, packed in by the hundreds into each building. All the different lives taking place in such a small space, living side by side, above and below.

In the food markets, customers were steadily gathering, haggling with butchers over carcasses hung from dripping walls or sizing up flapping fish in buckets of shallow water. People rushed around to get to their destinations, moody, uncooperative to the point the hostility began to resonate within me. As I was lining up my shots, I'd be pushed and shoved. They simply wanted me out of their way, which could be a struggle with the masses accumulating in places like the subways or shopping malls.

By mid-morning I found my way to an area where the streets were lined with florists. The owners fashioned and rearranged bouquets of auspicious blossoms or stacked luck-bringing houseplants. Every shade of colour was on display, every floral fragrance imaginable in the air. This was perfect, especially if I could get one of the group to hand a local girl a rose as she passed by. What a great shot that would be.

They were due here in two days' time and I prayed for sunshine if only for that one day. All being well Danny would arrive tomorrow. We'd scored a lucrative contract with the record company we landed in Germany who were so impressed with our work, they passed over all design and photography into our capable hands for a boyband called Daylight. This would be the start of something big for us if we got it right. It was an exciting time for Calibre Creative and I was living every second to the full, doing everything I could have dreamed of doing since I was a boy.

The bird market wasn't so easy to capture. I was shooed away any time I raised my camera and signs were clear that no photography was allowed, so this was out of the question. I was glad though, with so many birds stuffed into each individual cage, no amount of coverage would condone the cruelty. Instead, I headed for the Kowloon Street markets overflowing with clothes and apparel stalls, imagining the boys lined up with shoppers flowing past. And then onto Jade Market; one of the band members picking out an item of jewellery for a make-believe love interest in mind. This was all heaven, my imagination bursting at the seams.

After dinner in a dim sum bar, I walked the streets some more, envisioning the guys sitting on the steps of the Hong Kong Cultural Centre or mimicking the Bruce Lee statue in the Avenue of the

Stars. Finally, as night fell, I set up my tripod and put the camera into long exposure to absorb the lights of the skyscrapers and Ferris wheel of Victoria Harbour.

I had a couple of hours leisure time training at a local Wing Chun School in Mong Kok and by the time I returned to the hotel, I was exhausted. I collapsed onto the bed, ordered room service and shortly after phoning Louise and Emma, I was blissfully swept off to sleep.

Danny woke me around six in the morning. Luggage in hand, he hadn't checked into his own room yet. It was straight down to work. We went through the previous day's shots, sorting what would be used and what ideas would be discarded. We still had another full day ahead of us. That evening we would meet the band for the first time, get to know them and their management over dinner and socialise in the city after. They wanted to break Asia and were already building quite a following. I wondered, tingling with excitement, what the coming night would bring.

The forecast for the next day was looking superb, my prayers would hopefully be answered. It was great to have Danny by my side. Despite the long flight, his mood was upbeat. He hated flying but loved business. This was his side of things; dealing with clients, the meet and greets and keeping everything running smoothly. Together we made an excellent team.

Danny had everything organised the second we stepped out from reception, including a suited driver at the ready with a flashy black Tesla. First off, we went to the Elements Shopping Mall with five zones themed around the Chinese elements of earth, fire, metal, water, and wood. In the right spot the group would look awesome against the backdrop of the surrounding skyscrapers. We took a light breakfast at the IFC Mall where the long hallways were perfect for atmospheric depth shots. The creamy curves and shiny glass of Pacific Place made yet more excellent interior backgrounds and finally before lunch, we squeezed into the Harbour City Mall in Kowloon.

We spent the afternoon checking out various street locations and reconfirmed our appointment first thing in the morning at The Peak, where we'd managed to get the boys into the attraction to overlook Victoria Harbour before the hordes of tourists would arrive. With a couple of hours to kill, Danny and I went back to the hotel to discuss the final locations and check our equipment in preparation for the next day.

We arrived at the The Ritz-Carlton where the band members and their management were staying. On the 102nd floor was Tin Lung Heen, meaning Dragon in the Sky. Possibly the classiest restaurant I'd ever stepped foot in. I was in awe of the glittering views of Hong Kong harbour far below. Christian, Matt, Liam, and Ritchie were in their late teens/early twenties and filled to the brim with ego. However, they gelled with us from the outset and conversation flowed over wine and incredible Cantonese cuisine. We spoke about the locations we intended to photograph them at as dishes of barbecued pork covered in osmanthus honey, fried wagyu beef with bell peppers, steamed garoupa fillet with Jin Hua ham and sautéed lobster with bean curd were passed around and shared amongst us.

Danny had sorted out more staff for the day to help us and provide make up and wardrobe for the boys. When final details were concreted into place, and the meal was at an end, the boys asked us if we would like to go with them around the city for a couple of hours.

These guys could drink. Already they'd finished four bottles of highly expensive wine between them and wanted to hit the sake bars of Mong Kok, much to the management's disapprovals. I hadn't touched the wine, and as Danny and I took separate elevators from the group to meet them at the ground floor, he pointed out that I might have to have a couple of drinks to stay in good favour. I tried to protest, but for the sake of business relationships, on this occasion I'd have to relent.

The busy neon nightlife of Mong Kok was a complete contrast to the deserted morning streets that greeted me when I first arrived. It was almost impossible to move amongst the hordes of people that packed the roads. The management had retired to their rooms and left the boys in the hands of their security, Don, and Toby. I welcomed their presence as we huddled together trying to find space to walk.

We finally found a decent bar where the boys ordered the drinks. Danny insisted on paying for the evening's entertainment and ordered a round of Sake Ritas, with lemonades upon request for the security. I asked the boys how life had changed for them since they became famous. They had to be up at the crack of dawn for interviews, promotional events, gigs, rehearsals, meet and greets and signings day in day out. It was non-stop, but they weren't complaining, well not at this early stage of their careers. I could see it all going to their heads if their record sales were anything to go by. They were already huge on the iTunes and Spotify charts. When these guys drifted away from Danny and I, off into their own world again, our financial path would be set.

They kept encouraging me to drink more as I was being left way behind. I was steadily getting wasted. It wasn't a world I was comfortable in; the noise, the alcohol, the people, but somehow, I held it together. Danny slapped me on the back as I staggered back to my room.

'Well done, mate, you were a legend. I didn't think you were going to handle it at one point, but you pulled it all back. Just to let you know before you go to bed, their manager Lance called and said the boys really liked us and insisted on us working with them again in the future.' I shot a crooked smile his way, said that was great and closed the door behind me, eager to call Emma before I passed out.

The day couldn't have gone better. The sun was out, the sky a clear blue and Daylight, despite the amount they drank, were sharp and on time. They were totally professional on the shoots, posing perfectly to our direction and giving their best to the camera. They messed around a bit, but that was mainly to rile up their security and see how far they could push them. At one point, when we were at the dizzy heights of The Peak overlooking the island and the skyscrapers below, Ritchie got up on the railings and leaned too far back but was caught by Don at the last second. I didn't envy his job of doubling up as a babysitter in the slightest.

The sun set gloriously behind them on the dimming streets of Kwun Tong. A few long exposure shots with light streams of traffic around them with the silhouetted hills and lit skyscrapers above. The perfectionist I am with my work, even I was impressed with the results. And in true movie style, I concluded the day by calling out, 'That's a wrap, guys,' to a round of applause from us all.

After hugs and handshakes, they climbed into an awaiting luxury coach to take them to an all-star charity benefit while Danny and I packed up our kit and gave thanks to our temporary staff who had aided us throughout the day.

I met with Danny over coffee the following morning,

still pinching ourselves with how we managed to pull it all off so well. Our flight was at lunchtime, and with most of our gear packed, we had a little time left before we'd have to leave the hotel. Lance called Danny late last night. He'd spoken to their sister company, and if we could fit them in to our list of clients, they had four extra acts they would like us to consider working with. This trip was going from great to awesome, I couldn't believe our luck. We'd sent over a few sample pictures to Lance, and he was impressed to say the least.

By the time we were seated on the flight home, we could hardly keep still with the thrill of it all. Danny gently snored by my side as we were mid-way through the journey. I looked over to him, feeling blessed that I had such a good friend and such a wonderful family despite all the troubles that brought me to this point. If ever there was a God, I believed in him now.

The first thing I'd do when I got home was book another trip to Disneyland for Emma and treat her to a shopping trip at Bluewater. Danny took the wheel and drove us out of the airport and homeward bound. I dug my phone from my pocket and called Emma.

'Hello?'

'Hi Louise, we're on our way back now, should be with you in about an hour or so. Put Em on for me please.'

'Of course. All went well then?'

'Better than we could have dreamed.'

'Oh, that's great news. I was just about to tuck her into bed. She's just finished brushing her teeth. Here you go Emma.'

'Hello?'

'Hey you. Wow, you've brushed your teeth. The car smells all minty fresh. Danny, can you smell that?'

'It's making my eyes water, Em,' Danny called over.

'Ha-ha, you make me laugh, Daddy. Where are you?'

'About an hour away darling, we're just on the motorway now. I told you I'd be home soon.'

'Yay! I can't wait to see you. Is uncle Danny coming over too?'

'Maybe, we'll see. How about if you ask Aunty Louise if you can stay up until I come home? Or maybe you would rather see me in the morning?'

'No way. Aunty Louise, can I stay up for Daddy? Cool, Aunty Louise says I can stay up.'

'Okay sweetheart, I'll see you when I get back.'

'Okay. Love you, Daddy.'

We exited the motorway and headed for Sandgate as Danny placed Daylight's *Urban Mysteries* CD into the stereo. 'Got a signed copy,' he grinned.

I found myself singing along with him.

'How do I know this shit so well. Bloody hell, it's catchy,' I shouted above the ballad, *Lost City of Love*. Just then my phone rang, 'It's Louise, turn it down mate.' I slid open the call.

'Ben, where are you?'

'Right around the corner. We'll be with you in a minute.'

'Kirsten's taken Emma. I don't know what to do. I tried everything I could do to stop them, but she pushed me to the ground.'

'Slow down. What happened?'

She began to cry, 'She came to the door a couple of minutes ago with Tel. She started ranting about how she was going to get full custody now she'd met some rich guy she's been personal training.'

'It's alright Louise. Keep talking, I'm nearly home.'

'Emma came to the door with all the commotion and Tel grabbed her and bundled her into the back of Kirsten's car.'

'Where do you think they've gone?'

'I'm guessing to Tel's, but Ben...'

'I'm here now. We'll head over to Tel's first. Sit tight.'

I ended the call and instructed Danny of the route, informing him on the way what was happening. It wasn't that far to Tel's house, but I willed Danny to drive as fast as he could. I needed to get to Emma. She would be so scared, and she was really looking forward to seeing me. How could Kirsten, after all this time, think she should suddenly be the one to have custody of Emma? It was absurd. What was she thinking grabbing her like that?

As we cornered a dark country bend, Danny slammed on the brakes and brought the car to a stop on a grass verge. On the opposite side of the road was a red mini, smashed into a tree, smoke funnelling from the bonnet.

I jumped out of the car and ran over to the wreckage, 'Emma!'

I saw Kirsten outside the passenger door. She was shouting into the car at Tel, 'Stay in the driver's seat. I'm way over the limit. If the police find out I was the one driving, I'm screwed.'

'Where's Emma?' I screamed at her.

'Ben?'

'Where is Emma?'

'In the back. What are you doing here?' she slurred.

Emma was sprawled across the back. One of her legs was bent at a nasty angle, trapped under the seat in front of her. Blood was pouring from the top of her head as she lay unconscious in her *Frozen* pyjamas. She didn't even have a seatbelt on. My mind was in a spin. The driver's door was crushed, but the passenger door was open. I tried to yank the seat forward, but it was jammed.

I could hear Danny behind me. 'Oh no you don't,' he shouted to Kirsten. I guess she was trying to make a run for it, but I was too frantic to care.

'Danny, forget her, give me a hand with the seat.'

There was a murmur and then an excruciating cry as Emma came to. Her little face: she didn't know what was going on. I kept pulling at the seat. And then flames erupted from the engine area, at once ripping through the dashboard. Tel tried to get free, but he was too weak from his own injuries. He flailed his scorching arms around and yelled as the inferno licked at his skin. Fire spread rapidly, completely filling the car with intense heat and smoke. I hit the back window in a futile attempt to break it as Emma cried her heart out looking on so helpless, confusion and fear contorting her face.

'Daddy, daddy,' she screamed.

A bang and a whoosh of fire engulfed the entire interior. Danny pulled me back.

'No! Emma! Emma!' I screamed.

Her little blackened hands clawed at the window and then fell away, disappearing at the mercy of the flames.

I ran back, screaming her name, but Danny tackled me to the ground, 'She's gone, mate,' he wept into my ear. 'She's gone.'

17

I check into a hotel, take the key card and head out to a barbershop recommended to me by the girl on reception. Before me, my long dark hair falls to the ground and my beard is swept away by the blade of a cutthroat razor. I stare at the coldness in my eyes in the mirror. Each plan I made, every time I imagined Kirsten dead at my hands, had all amounted to nothing. The stress had built over the last few weeks, to yet another pinnacle and I had mistakenly thought that I could cope with it all. In truth, I could barely handle the next second. I'm pathetic and riddled beyond all repair. Had I not accelerated into a wall of intoxication at such speed, maybe, just maybe, I could have controlled my world more competently. But minute after minute I see Emma's face lost in that hell. Night after night I hear her screaming and I just can't forgive myself for not being able to save her. And day after day I cannot condone the justice system for not imprisoning Kirsten, for believing her lies and putting it all down to a tragic accident.

I contemplate the man I was, kind, smart, confident, and successful. Staring back at my own reflection now, with that faraway look in my eyes, I know I will never be him again. The worst part of me I thought never existed is all that I have left. I realise we're not who we think we are and what we cannot forgive, we sometimes become.

As I step into the sunlight, I put my phone to my ear and hope that Amy picks up. After several rings, she answers.

'Hi Amy, it's Ben. Can we meet?'

'Ben? I didn't think I'd hear from you again. Where are you?'

'Bangkok. I know I probably don't deserve it, but can we talk?'

'Of course, it'd be lovely to see you. Do you want me to come to you or you to me?'

'Tell me where you are, and I'll be there.'

I jot down the location of her hotel on the west bank of the Chao Phraya River. She's waiting patiently outside the sliding glass doors, head buried in her tablet. I approach her, but she looks straight past me.

'Hey,' I say with a shy smile.

'Hi. Um, I'm waiting for someone.' She focuses in, puzzled for a second, 'Ben?'

'I guess you probably won't like me now I've spruced myself up.'

'Oh no, you look very nice. So much better without the beard. I did always wonder what you'd look like under there.'

We pass the gawking statues and towering temple grounds of Wat Arun and catch a ferry across the river for something to eat. I want to hang on every word she says, take my mind away from last night and be lost to her radiance again.

Finding a seat in McDonald's, Amy relays how Bentley robbed Zoe, and how she had to lend her the money for a flight home. She doesn't think she'll ever see her again. She asks about what I've been up to, and I invite her back to my hotel so we can talk.

There I sit her opposite me on the bed. I owe her an explanation, it's the least I can do. I have nothing to lose and if she's the person I wholeheartedly believe she is, then what we have between us could be a real possibility. I only hope she can forgive my actions without casting too much of a shadow of judgement over me.

I tell her how I met Danny, all about Kirsten, everything about Emma and my last conversations with her in Hong Kong and all that followed. The devastating heartache of packing away Emma's things and an eternity of never coming to terms with saying goodbye. The months of darkness where I hid behind closed curtains, refusing the suffocating sympathy from family and friends and the selfish burden I buried myself under, the only thing left I could call my own. How I lost myself to drugs and the bottle; my charred lungs sucked dry, and my liver cooked and served up on a platter. How I was so far out of everyone's reach of normal, secluding myself and never speaking of my depression, just hiding behind a facade, and allowing it to tear away at the very fabric of my soul. And then I tell her why I'm in Thailand, holding nothing back. And that it was a year yesterday since Emma died.

I wait for her to wipe her tears and the look of shock from her face, stand and leave, even report me to the police, but she simply takes me by the hand, squeezing it tightly and says she understands.

'I knew you were suffering, but I could never have guessed it was anything that awful. Remember I've lost a great deal too and went down the same path as you. A person is less likely to judge others for their mistakes if they've learnt from their own. Had I watched my daughter die in such a horrific way, then yes, I would have probably acted the same. You're human, Ben, nothing more, nothing less. But you must try and find a way forward, to forgive yourself, if not for you, for the memory of Emma. I'm sure by what you've told me she loved you very much and would be deeply unhappy to see you this way.'

For the first time in months the tears fall uncontrollably, and I look away.

'Don't be ashamed to cry, Ben. It's sometimes the only way we can cleanse such tragedy in our lives.'

She reaches forward and wraps her arms around

me. I can feel the warm damp of her own tears on my neck. When she leans back, she smiles, 'If you're willing enough, I'd love to share my life with you and maybe we can start again, rewrite this story so we can both have a happy ending.'

'I'd like that.'

As we gather ourselves together, she invites me to stay a while in England with her and says she'll cancel her flight for tomorrow morning so we can travel together. She'll go back to her hotel and collect her things, tie up a few loose ends and be back at eight to stay the night with me.

When she goes, I'm left to my silence. I breathe heavy as if I've spent half of my life drowning and I've finally resurfaced. But the stress pounds me back under when I see Danny light up on my phone.

'You're in Bangkok?' He's breaking up and I can hardly hear him.

'Yeah. Where are you?'

'Bangkok. We need to talk.'

'Do we? Can't we just leave it for a while?'

'No, we need to clear the air and discuss some things straight away. I want you to meet me at the Sathorn Unique Tower. There will be a driver with you in ten minutes.'

I let out a deep sigh, 'I'll see you there.'

Although I must have dropped him in it with Kirsten, I'm seething that he could have had an affair with the woman that killed my daughter. She took everything from me and he's carrying on with her as if nothing ever happened. I'm overwhelmed with a sudden rage that consumes me, more than likely as a result of going back over it all with Amy.

18

Outside a silver Mercedes hums in neutral. An Indian driver in his forties gets out, walks over, and addresses me, 'I am Aarav. You are Mr Ben, sir?'

'Oh God, not you as well.'

He cocks an eyebrow, 'Sorry sir?'

He opens the back door, but I get in the front.

'So, Aarav, do you know Danny well?'

'Oh yes, sir. Very good man is Mr Danny, sir.'

Along a side street from a bustling main road lined with businesses, he cuts the engine, gets out and guides me under a bent back piece of corrugated iron that supposedly protects the building from intruders. I stop to look up at the grey skeleton soaring above. 'It's a bit spooky.'

'Ha, yes, sir. It is having nickyname, Ghost Tower. Please follow me, sir, many steps to climb. We are to be on rooftop, take much time. Please tread very carefully and let me be leading the way.'

At first the ascent is easy going, but soon becomes a huge task to my weathered lungs. I ask to take a breather and enquire if we're nearly there.

'Oh no, sir, maybe only quarter way.'

In some places the staircase is in complete darkness, and with no handrails, I am thankful for Aarav's guidance and torch. Partially flooded hallways appear on every landing, crumbling balconies leading from the empty rooms.

'What is this place?' I ask.

'It is unfinished skyscraper. It is being high-rise luxury apartments, but construction is stopped because of 1997 financial crises. Building has many bad luck. Body of Swedish man also found hanged on 43rd floor. He is committing suicide, sir.'

'So why does Danny want me to meet him here?'

'This I cannot say. I am only bringing you to location.'

By the time we eventually reach the top, I'm on the verge of collapse. But a wave of adrenalin courses through me as I catch sight of Danny looking out over the vast corners of the city.

Aarav waggles his head and leaves the way he came.

'Danny,' I shout. It takes everything in me not to push him over the edge.

He strolls up to me and proffers his hand, 'Ben, you look well. I'm glad you came. This is about the only place in Bangkok where the walls don't have ears.'

I can't take any more. I push him so hard he falls to the floor. I follow up with a kick to his ribs. He cries out, grabs my foot, and tugs it, sending me off balance. I'd forgotten he'd learnt Brazilian Jiu Jitsu in the marines and before I know it, I'm on my back, his leg over my throat, my arm locked in both of his. I cry out as he increases the tension in my elbow and shoulder.

'Promise me you'll calm down, Ben. I know you're angry, but you need to let me explain.'

'Screw you,' I gurgle. He pulls harder, 'Okay, Okay.'

The pressure lightens as he releases his grip. I slump down against a wall, rubbing my neck and massaging my shoulder.

He sits beside me, the traffic echoing far below.

'It's too hot for this crap, Ben. I thought bringing you up all those steps would have knackered you out.'

'What do you want to tell me, Danny? How you've been screwing my ex and the murderer of my child?'

'I said I had to get close to her, remember. The only way to win her trust was to say I'd severed all ties with you and that I wanted revenge for you robbing me out my half of the business.'

'Robbing you? What?'

'I had to convince her. Emma was like a daughter to me too. I was there, remember? I would have taken care of all this long ago myself if you weren't so bloody insistent. I knew you weren't cut out for this so I kept stalling you so you'd be reminded of what Kirsten was like, so you could store up enough venom to take her down on the day of the wedding.'

I stare at my feet, 'Go on.'

'It took a while for her to believe me. I said that I wanted to take all the money from Calibre's account and place into an account in the Caymans, and would she be interested in making a fortune with me. She was intrigued. I told her I could make a hefty amount in investments if she seeped some of the cash from the personal account Rodrigo had set up for her. She was a bloody natural, mate. She had him wrapped around her finger.'

'But that doesn't explain why you were sleeping with her.'

'She was becoming suspicious, so I had to make her fall in love with me. And she did. I spun her a dream of an alternative life together. But it got way out of hand. She wasn't satisfied with the amount she was transferring so she got him to propose to her. When the suggestion of a prenuptial agreement came up, she flipped and threatened to leave him, and of course he caved. After two years she was going to bleed him dry.'

'But why, Danny? You've got enough money.'

'As you know she only thinks in pound signs, it was the only way to get into her head. But I did have another reason. She owed you thousands from the amount she took from you financially. She owed you millions with what she took from you emotionally.'

I swung round to face him, 'I don't need her

money or yours or Rodrigo's.'

'I know, but it's yours, nonetheless. I've transferred the money into an account in your name. There's close to a million in there.'

'Keep it. It's not going to bring Emma back.'

'Of course it's not mate, I'm fully aware of that. But it's a start to a new life.'

'Have you not seen the state I've been in? Do you think that money is really going to help me?'

'It's there and it'll stay there, that's all I'm saying. Bloody hell, mate, there was never any remorse, guilt, or regret for what she did. She carried on as she always did, not caring, and hurting people for her own gain, no matter the cost.'

'I'm not going to thank you for this. Emma's dead and Kirsten is still out there.'

'Which leads me on to this...'

He pulls his phone from his pocket, swipes the screen, and passes it to me. Staring back is a news report posted this morning:

Newly-wed Wife of Tycoon Missing in Gulf of Thailand

Property tycoon Rodrigo D'Souza's newly-wed wife, Kirsten D'Souza (formerly Ableman), has tragically fallen from their luxury superyacht off the coast of Phuket in Thailand...

I hand the phone back and stand, 'What is this Danny, some kind of sick joke?'

'No joke, brother. She fell from the Astondoa last

night.'

'You're messing with me?'

'Nope.'

'What happened?'

'After you lost your bottle...'

'I didn't lose my bottle. The safety got stuck and then one of her goons showed up.'

'Well, after you messed it all up, she came back aboard, found me and started making a scene about how she'd just seen you.' We meet eyes and I then stare over his shoulder to the graffiti plastered walls. 'Anyway, I calmed her down by marching her outside, letting her have a spliff and snort a couple of lines. I persuaded her to have me stay on board when they set sail. I get on famously with Rodrigo and he's got no idea what's going on behind his back. He agreed after she said she wanted me to come along for a while.'

'And?'

'Later on, when he passed out from drinking too much, we were out sitting on the steps on the back of the yacht talking and having a smoke. She got up to stretch as the boat hit a choppy wave. She stumbled and I simply put my foot in her back.'

'You pushed her over?'

He stays silent for a moment. 'She's out of your life, Ben. Shark bait. That's what you wanted wasn't it?'

'Yes, but...'

'But what?'

'I don't know. I think I would have regretted it if I'd killed her.'

'Well, you didn't, mate. I'm the one who spent the night consoling Rodrigo and I'm the one who dealt with all the questions from the police. They're not treating the death as suspicious and it's doubtful her body will ever be found, despite the amount of search units assigned. I went to bed straight after I pushed Kirsten. Rodrigo knocked on my door an hour later enquiring after her. I'd said I last saw her sitting at the end of the yacht.'

I can't soak it all in. I've had enough to deal with already without this to add another layer.

'Danny, I need time to think. I'll call you later.'

'Take all the time you need. But one last thing, before you start feeling any guilt over this, because I know you will, remember, not once did she express any kind of sorrow over Emma. She openly admitted to me the only time she ever worried was when her head was on the chopping block over leaving the scene of the accident. If you have any guilt over Kirsten's death, you need to have your head tested, mate.'

I look down and then back to him as I reach the stairwell doorway, 'I'll see you later, Danny.'

Aarav is waiting five floors below in the darkness. He switches on his torch and guides me down the stairs and back to the car.

In my room I fall to the bed. I thought I'd feel something more, a sense of relief, exhilaration even, but when Danny told me, I felt nothing but regret, that she, like Emma, was gone. I'd spent so long hating her for what she'd done that when he broke the news of her "accident", I felt as if a part of me had died with her. In the darkest corner of my heart, Kirsten was all that I had left of Emma, and although it was filled with so much vengeance, it was all I had to keep me going.

My phone pings a message from Amy, 'Be with you just after eight. Got us some tickets to leave at midnight if you still want to.'

I reply, 'Great, I'm just going to have a rest before we set off.' I finish with, 'Thank you Amy, for everything.'

She writes back in seconds, 'We'll talk soon x.'

I remove the Mekhong from my bag, unscrew the lid and drink deeply. I'm desperate for some sleep. The failure to calculate all the crap flying from every angle is making my head spin. I prop the phone up, tap on Manchester Orchestra's *The Silence*, put it on loop and begin to sob.

I steady the glass aloft, catching the amber glint of the bare lightbulb in the unsteady waves of alcohol lapping for my weakness. I feign a grin, knock it back, holding it down against my body's quivering protest. Staring up at me like little dead soldiers, forty or so pills lay in wait for an uncertain trial to acidity. I've never experienced a calm such as this, a solace I only wish went with me as a lifelong companion. Both worst enemy and best friend have finally merged, showing no mercy.

I lose count of how many glasses I drain and how many pills I take, but the warmth is so comforting, the sleep so tempting that I give in to the soft light my eyes close around. I hear the door opening, and there on the threshold she stands, her face filled with a smile, 'Daddy, you're home!'

Thank you for reading What We Become

If you have any thoughts you would like to share or require any further information about this book or any past or future projects, please visit my website www.reecewillis.com

Alternatively you can find me on Goodreads, Facebook @reecewillisauthor and Instagram @rwillisauthor

If you enjoyed this book, a rating/review at the place of purchase would be greatly appreciated.

Also by Reece Willis

Towards the Within

Sometimes the further you distance yourself, the closer you are to the truth.

What starts out as a simple trip around India soon becomes a psychological journey into the darkness of Sam's past. One he knows there's no running from.

When Sam decides to give up his mundane life and travel to India, he has no idea what he'll do when he gets there and it isn't long before his lack of preparation takes its toll.

Vulnerable and alone, Sam is haunted by memories of his childhood and as he struggles to make sense of the pain he has suffered he follows a dangerous path that has devastating consequences.

Behind the Shadows:

The Writing Process of What We Become

The writing of What We Become commenced in late 2017, once the final draft of Towards the Within was complete. Initially it was a small idea of obsession with the main character pursuing his lost love across Thailand, but as the early drafts developed, the story blossomed into something so much bigger. The conclusion was the first section of the story I had in mind with everything else centred around this idea.

The story opens up with the song *Closer* by Kings of Leon. I trawled through my iPod to find a suitable piece to commence Ben's journey, and found *Closer* to be a superb start with such a poignant theme for his path. Music is an integral part of my life. Most of my memories are bookmarked and easily accessed by a piece of music should I wish to travel back to a certain aspect of my past, and often I'm caught off guard by a song which can trigger a recollection I may have forgotten. I like to think Ben held himself together with the comfort and solace his music collection provided him. It's often been a source of escape for me when times have been tough.

Ben's character to a degree is based on elements of my past, especially his struggles with mental health. With the patience and support from my family I have long overcome my anxieties. These days I'm very happy and live a clean and healthy lifestyle. But I know only too well how post traumatic stress disorder can take hold and erode one's soul, appearing unexpectedly at a moment's notice.

It was great to revisit Thailand, a favourite of the countries I have travelled, along with Hong Kong. I have some wonderful memories of Bangkok, Chiang Mai and Phuket and the beautiful people who reside in these special places. I also have a close connection with Sandgate, Hythe and Seabrook in South East England and it was a pleasure to write these personal locations into the book. What was also nice was to include my love of photography and Martial Arts as recurring themes throughout the story-line. I have practised Karate, Judo, Muay Thai Kickboxing and for the last fifteen years, Jeet Kune Do and Wing Chun Kung Fu.

It's been very emotional writing What We Become, and at times I found myself close to tears, being utterly absorbed into Ben's world. As with all of the characters in my books, it's hard to walk away from them, having been completely invested and committed to the conviction of their development.

The story closes with *The Silence*. Manchester Orchestra is one of my favourite bands and the song seemed a perfect way to end Ben's traumatic journey.

Printed in Great Britain
by Amazon